The Alfred Book of Ghastly Tales

Volume II

The Alfred Book of Ghastly Tales
Volume II

EDITED WITH AN INTRODUCTION BY
Monica Nowik

WHITLOCK PUBLISHING
Alfred, NY

First Whitlock Publishing edition 2021

Whitlock Publishing
Alfred, NY

Editorial matter
© Monica Nowik

Front cover image
© Kaitlin "Katt" Villanueva

Photographs
© S. K. Sage

ISBN: 978-1-943115-47-1

This book was set in Adobe Garamond Pro on 55# acid-free
paper that meets ANSI standards for archival quality.

ACKNOWLEDGEMENTS

Thank you to Dr. Allen Grove for inviting me to work on this project and guiding me through the process. I have learned so much about editing, publishing, and more.

Thank you to Laurie Lounsberry Meehan for all the help and information she provided for the introduction. It was truly a pleasure to chat about ghosts and legends.

Finally, I am eternally grateful to my family and friends who listened to every small concern of mine throughout this project. You know who you are.

NOTE ON THE TEXT

The stories in this anthology are loosely based on Alfred, New York folklore. This is a work of fiction. All events or incidents are fictitious. All historical information provided by the Alfred University Archives and Alfred local newspapers.

TABLE OF CONTENTS

ILLUSTRATIONS

INTRODUCTION

A N INFAMOUSLY HAUNTED dormitory known as the Brick. An obscure town with an even foggier past. A foreboding castle that lurks on a hill. Parting our way through a thick shroud of woods and forestry, we once again stumble upon Alfred University, situated in Allegany County, New York. Here is an all-new collection of delightfully spooky ghost stories from university students and faculty focused on the university and its surroundings.

In the first volume of *The Alfred Book of Ghastly Tales,* we took a trip into the chilling past of Alfred, featuring historical events from the founding of the Village in 1808 and the university in 1836, to the campus-turned-infirmary during both World Wars, to Sally the Skeleton and the Black Knight. Though Alfred has grown and evolved over the years, haunting tales continue to be whispered around campus. Let's investigate Alfred University as it appears today and take a look at what has spurred on the imaginations of students and citizens for centuries, causing them to envision ghastly happenings. Just what is it about the picturesque Alfred that inspires...well, fear?

Alfred University's rural location near the Pennsylvania border doesn't appear on many maps. Its isolation makes it the ideal setting for horror stories, especially those taking place in rural areas. Early examples of horror can be seen in ancient Greek and Roman culture: Pliny the Younger, a 1st century Roman author and politician, wrote a story about a haunted house, and Greek mythology is chock full of horrific imagery, such as in the tales of Eurydice, the Minotaur, Medusa, and many others. Myths and folklore pervaded the world long before anyone thought of making it into a category set apart from other fiction. Specifically, horror literature may be responsible for our fascination with the macabre to this very day; in the English language, it rose into its own art form at the end of the 18th century, which we can see in Horace Walpole's *The Castle of Otranto* (1764) and Matthew Lewis's *The Monk* (1796). From this period stems "Gothic horror," common in the 18th and 19th centuries, a genre of horror fiction that emphasizes dark, gloomy settings. Gothic horror explored concepts such as perverseness, man's hubris, and the concept of the "sublime," a term associated with a feeling of wonder, or being overwhelmed.

As horror matured, stories wishing to terrify readers found new ways to do so. The 20th century began with H.P. Lovecraft, found Shirley Jackson in the middle, and ended in an explosion of slasher films and Stephen King bestsellers; horror had become a way to comment upon feminism, repression, and other social issues. Among the many different subgenres that manifested during the last one hundred years was "folk horror," or "rural horror."

Stories falling into this category were nothing new, but Piers Haggard, director of *The Blood on Satan's Claw* (1971), is credited with the first use of the term "folk horror" to encapsulate the subgenre and bring attention to it in 2004, though director and screenwriter Mark Gatiss later popularized it. This kind of horror tends to rely on isolated, rural settings, such as in small towns or in the woods, and plays largely off psychological horror—think *Children of the Corn* (1977) or *A Quiet Place* (2018). Religious or cult-like themes are often prevalent.

Why do we find rural horror so creepy? And why does Alfred seem to eerily follow the conventions of the subgenre? The main components of rural horror, and indeed, some glaringly obvious aspects of Alfred itself, can be broken down into three parts. Perhaps upon further inspection, we can come to understand why people today, and why people almost two hundred years ago, believed that Alfred University might be infested with ghosts.

ISOLATION

Isolation may be the singular most important theme required for rural horror. Complete isolation is not, of course, necessary; the story need only take place in some secluded setting, usually so that the characters, and by proxy the audience, are far away from any kind of real help. Inhabitants describe Alfred as "out in the middle of nowhere," as it is 20 minutes from Hornell, the nearest small city, and even farther from the nearest big city, Rochester, almost 80 miles away.

Within Alfred itself, you might experience a jarring separation from the outside world. Walking alone at night, it's impossible not to feel as if you're being watched; even though the campus is silent, you may think you hear footsteps behind you. The soundscape is unplagued by nearby highways or loud city parties; the most you might hear is the distant shouts of the football team practicing on the field. Some areas of campus are quite literally in a state of decay, such as South Hall, which has stood abandoned and falling into ruin since 1995 and is the setting for S.K. Sage's "South Hall." Other locations may still be in use, but because of how far away they are from the hubbub of campus, they feel deserted and forsaken; the Observatory serves as a good example, setting the tone of seclusion and fear for Eleanor Fanning's "Lost Things Found, Found Things Lost."

Many of the suites reside far away from the noise of Main Street, unlike the other dormitories. Built in the woods, Anne's House is home to residents who have reported seeing red eyes and a feeling that there was a malignant spirit dwelling there. Those living in Openhym have also allegedly witnessed the red eyes, though there is no historical basis for why an evil spirit might inhabit these residence halls.

Supernatural phenomena on campus are more likely to take place in the Brick, which acted as a temporary infirmary for wounded soldiers during World War I and II, as well as a hospital for victims of the 1918 influenza pandemic and saw several of these patients pass away during their time there. Six of our authors—Kaitlin "Katt" Villanueva, S.K. Sage, Kazimeras Taggert, Noah T. Howard, Dr. Juliana Gray and Robert Giancarlo—have set stories in this residence hall. Students in the Brick have described the long hallways and winding staircases as feeling "empty," even when the building is full of people. In Howard's "Another Brick in the Wall" and Giancarlo's "Nightmare on Park Street," both narrators experience unexplained phenomena, despite the presence of roommates and friends. Said to be the most haunted building on campus, the Brick's residents say that they have heard people pacing the hallways, walking on the roof and rattling their doorknobs when there appears to be no one around; in Taggert's "The Night Round," doors slam on their own and mysterious figures disappear into thin air. Personal belongings go missing often in the Brick: in one student's case, they had lost their wallet, only to hear a disembodied voice say, *"Look in the drawer."* Upon inspecting said drawer, the student found their wallet.

A Small Town

Folk horror authors are fond of using small towns and communities to create a watchful atmosphere. Usually in this kind of setting, the inhabitants of said social group have lived there their entire lives; their strange ways may seem unsettling to the onlooker, but not to them. The movie *Midsommar* (2019) puts this concept to good use, as do the works of M. R. James who wrote his short stories around the turn of the 20th century.

The township of Alfred, with its population of just over 5,000, passes our "small town" test with flying colors. Though today's residents are mostly warm and welcoming, it's understandable that an "outsider" may feel unsettled by how closely knit the town is. If you're unfamiliar with the Village, you might become paranoid and feel monitored or judged from behind the drawn curtains. Throughout the area, many buildings have towers that rise above the rest, such as the church steeple and the tower of Alumni Hall. Who knows what could be watching from its perch? Who knows what sinister happenings could be going on behind closed doors? In Juno Tangry's "Walled In," the narrator finds the local neighbors unwelcoming, and unearths an old, ugly secret hiding within the Village.

The town itself has a ghastly history even without taking the university into account. Sledding accidents, epidemics, and murder took place in the Village of Alfred; some claim that these events did not transpire without leaving a ghostly trace, and in Josie Fasolino's "The Donation," the narrator experiences a gruesome event right on Main Street. Jane Brooks was found guilty in the murder of her lover's wife in 1863, and before being executed, President Allen of Alfred University bought her skeleton for the purposes of scientific study. The first woman to be convicted of murder in Allegany County, Jane Brooks's remains came to be known as Sally the Skeleton; she disappeared from the campus sometime in the middle of the 1900's, and her whereabouts are currently unknown.

In addition to the vanished Sally's transgression, another tale of murder still floats around the community. Legend has it that an old pool of water behind a former Alfred fraternity house originally had another house built upon it sometime after the Revolutionary War. The owner was digging out a cellar for his home when he struck water, flooding the house. A man arrived at the house a few days later, claiming to be a former suitor of the owner's wife. A fight ensued, and the owner pushed the newcomer down the stairs to his watery death in the cellar. The house no longer stands, but for unknown reasons, this location is still known as John's Pond. Since the 1940's students have "seen" a ghost walking across the water—perhaps it is the angry ghost of the murdered man.

Nature

Nature is not specific to rural horror, but rather a staple of the entire horror genre. How often does a group of friends head into the woods only to never appear again? From *Come Into My Parlor* (1948) by Manly Wade Wellman to the classic slasher film *Friday the 13th* (1980) to the horror-parody *Cabin in the Woods* (2011), the power of nature is a dominant theme in scary stories. There may be any number of things lurking behind the trees—serial killers, something that looks like a deer but isn't, or perhaps some other unspeakable terror. In Stephen King's *The Shining* (1977), the characters are at the mercy of natural elements due to the sheer amount of snow in the Colorado Rockies.

Alfred is indeed hit with frequent snowstorms, which often keep both students and faculty indoors in an icy quarantine. During the warmer months, this snow turns to rain and sometimes floods the Valley, leading to many historic natural disasters. Notable here is the New York State Flood of 1935 when an unusual mass of maritime air moved towards New York at the same time as a mass of polar continental air. Upon meeting, they caused heavy rainfall; flooding caused at least 43 deaths and 25 million dollars in damage across the state. Earlier, in 1920, a cyclone swept Allegany County, leaving "scarcely a house... undamaged" (*Andover News*, 1920). Alfred also has a long history of buildings burning down, since many of them are built entirely with wood; woodstoves and fireplaces, which were essential before the widespread integration of electricity, would have sparked more than few flames. The first recorded house built in the Valley burned down in 1819, most likely due to an irresponsible squatter.

Besides natural disasters, a calmer form of nature comes in the form of woodland animals. We are visited by the deer that share the property, as well as many other creatures from the woods that will surely cross your path. The hiking trail behind the university leads into the woods, which is the landscape for Dr. Shan K. Sundaram's "Glass Ghosts of Alfred"; it's a beautiful, lonely walk during the day and a nightmare-inducing one at night. The trees cast eerie shadows, and every snap of every twig keeps you alert. If you get onto Main Street and start heading south towards the Alfred Stables, the scenery will give way to farms and open fields; while the cows may be a reassuring sight, when the fields are empty, they can seem to swallow a person whole.

With such a rich history and a haunting atmosphere, it is little surprise that supernatural stories began to spring up around Alfred. Ghosts acted as an easy explanation for the unexplainable. Students in the 19th century may have told tales to scare their friends, who in turn came to believe that something truly haunted the university and town, and this is perhaps what led to the perceived "ghosts" that still supposedly walk the campus and surrounding area today. Or maybe not—maybe there *are* things beyond explanation.

Here lies Alfred, a town creeping with mystery and intrigue. Take a walk with the unreliable narrators of Wyatt Zindle's "Paper Thin" and Sydney Barnett's "Red Coat." Enter, if you will, into the dreamlike trances of Audrey Buddendeck's "I Died" and Emily Swendson's "Horror Class," or peer review a scientific experiment in Sophie Eckhardt's "A Study on *Alienus Terrestriosum* in the Alfred University Biology Department." Alfred is waiting: step in and enjoy our ghostly collection of stories—oh, and don't forget to check over your shoulder.

MONICA NOWIK, 2021
ALFRED, NY

The John L. Stull Observatory.

The observatory is home to one of the largest optical telescopes in
NY State, the Austin-Fellows 32 inch Newtonian Reflector.

LOST THINGS FOUND, FOUND THINGS LOST
ELEANOR FANNING

YOU'RE HALFWAY TO your dorm when you realize you left your phone in the Observatory. It's freezing and icy and dark and you don't *want* to go back, but you need your alarms to wake you up and keep you on schedule, and you need to be able to answer your mother if she texts, or else she'll freak out, and you want to be able to message your friends and check your email without pulling out your entire laptop. So, you heave a sigh and pat your pockets to make sure you still have the keys, at least, and wonder if you'd still have left your phone behind if the professor hadn't asked you to stay and lock up while she went off to a friend's birthday party or something. Perhaps your kindness will be your undoing, you think, then snort and shake your head at yourself as you turn around and walk back the way you came, placing your feet ever so carefully so you don't slip and fall. This is especially important when crossing the road from the apartments to the parking lot; you don't want to slide down the hill. Without your phone, if you fell and broke your legs out here, you may well freeze to death before you could call public safety or 911.

You make it to the Observatory driveway, shoulders hunched, fists shoved deep into your pockets, chin tucked against the wind, and you're just starting up it when you hear what sounds like crying. You look around, half nervous, half concerned, but the streetlamps in the parking lot illuminate nothing except the snow, and the woods and field to either side are cloaked in shadows, giving nothing away. The Observatory is dark, just as you left it, but the crying is coming from there.

If you didn't need your phone, the choice to continue would have been more difficult to make. But you do need your phone, and, you acknowledge grudgingly, you are worried that you might have accidentally locked a student in one of the telescope buildings. You don't know how such a thing could have happened, but what if it did? You refuse to go to prison for involuntary manslaughter. So, up the drive you go.

The crying—sobbing, really—is coming from the Orange Telescope, which does have the most potential hiding spots. You unlock the door and open it warily, then scowl into the darkness and try to remember where the light switch is in this building. Left of the door, maybe?

"Hello?" you say into the darkness as you feel around for the switch. The crying stops.

"H-Hello?" a wavering voice replies, and a light shines out of the darkness right into your eyes.

"Jesus Christ, turn that off! I'll have the lights on in a second, fuck," you complain. You find the red lights first but even a little bit helps, and the white lights are right beside them. Turning from the wall, you take in the tableau.

The crier appears to be a girl, a freshman probably, and she's sitting at the bottom of the stairs, back against the wall, snotty nosed and red-eyed, and bleeding from the head.

"Jesus Christ," you say again, stepping towards her. "What happened?"

"I-I I dro-opped the h-hatch o-on m-my head," the girl says, still sobbing, "a-and i-i-it *re-eally* hurt."

"*Fuck*," you say, and go for your phone before remembering you don't have it. "Do you have your phone on you?" you ask the girl, crouching down next to her.

"N-no, i-it fe-ell," she says, pointing vaguely to the side. You look over and don't see anything immediately, so you turn back to her.

"Hey," you say, trying to soften your voice, even though you're terrified. "What's your name?"

"I-I'm, um, So-Sophie," the girl cries. She hasn't met your eyes or really moved her head since you first saw her and it's worrying you.

"Okay, Sophie, hi. I'm the TA for Astronomy Lab. Do you remember me?"

"Y-yeah, you a-always h-help people w-with the l-labs."

"Alright, okay, yeah, yeah I do, good, you remember that, good." You take a moment to consider the likelihood of one of the students remembering your name and decide not to bother asking. "Okay, uh, do you remember what day it is?"

"Fe-February th-third, I th-think," the girl says, her sobs quieting a bit. "B-but it mi-ight b-be the fo-fourth b-by n-n-now," she adds as an afterthought.

"Yeah, okay, good. I think it is the fourth by now, but I don't have my phone to check," you say. She seems okay for the time being…You decide. "Okay, so, I'm going to go look for your phone, okay? So we can call public safety and 911 and get you all patched up. Does that sound good?"

"I-I g-guess," Sophie sniffles.

"Wonderful," you say, and go look for her phone under the stairs.

You spend five minutes, or maybe twenty, craning your neck around—truly, you have no sense of time, yet *another* reason you wish you had your phone with you— trying not to touch anything unless you absolutely have to before giving up and going back to Sophie, whose sobs have at this point ceased. She looks at you as you approach, and you're glad to see she has one hand held against the wound on her head. You'd forgotten to tell her to apply pressure, but she's doing it anyway.

"Y-you didn't find it t-then?" Sophie asks, only the slightest waver left in her voice.

"No, are you sure you dropped it when you fell? It could be upstairs still."

"I dunno. Maybe," Sophie says. She looks tired, well, of course she does, but you're worried all the same.

"I'll check upstairs," you say. "Hang tight."

She doesn't say anything in return, just sort of hums as you walk up the first flight of stairs to the landing. You don't see her phone, so you continue up, carefully pushing up the hatch and then closing it again behind you once you've used the light from below to locate the upstairs switches and turn them on. You look around the Orange Telescope and see nothing. Then, you do see something.

"What the fuck," you say, more because the silence has started to grate on your nerves than because it's strange to see that someone's propped their phone up on the ledge where the observatory dome meets the building itself.

You cross the room and pick up the phone, an older iPhone with a case covered in stickers, and try turning it on. The screen glows, the time 12:45 standing stark white against the dark hair of some anime character who's being used as the lock screen. You also see the small red six percent in the battery corner and swear under your breath. You leave the hatch open as you descend; you can always close it later.

"Can you put your password in for me Sophie? So we can call public safety?" You proffer her the phone, and she looks at you, confused.

"That's not mine," she says.

"I—What?" You look at the phone in your hand; it's not yours either. Did someone else really leave their phone here?

"I found mine, actually," Sophie says, showing you the phone in her hand, also an iPhone and also covered in stickers. "But it's dead," she adds before you can ask her if she's called public safety or 911 yet.

"Fuck, okay. Well, here, we can call 911 on this one, at least," you say, turning the phone on again. The battery says three percent and you bite back a curse.

"Nine-one-one, what's your emergency?" says the voice on the other end, and you could cry, you're so relieved.

"Hi! This girl I'm with got hit in the head and she's bleeding pretty bad, we're at—" is all you can say before the phone dies. "Motherfucker!" you spit, taking the phone down from your ear and glaring at the black screen.

"Oh, did it die too?" Sophie asks.

"Yeah, yeah, it *fucking* did," you say, then take a deep breath. "Okay. Okay. I'm going to go look for my phone. Will you be okay here? Are you okay? You look really pale."

"I'll be fine, I think. I could probably make it back to my dorm with a bit of help."

"Yeah, well, you also need to get checked for a concussion, so," you say. "Are you cold? It's freezing in here, and you haven't been moving for ages. Can you feel your fingers? Your toes?"

"I've been moving them," Sophie assures you. "I'll be fine, really. You can go look for your phone."

"Okay," you say dubiously, but you go.

The first building you look in is the classroom, just in case you never even took your phone into the telescopes to begin with. Also, because it's heated. But a scan around the room and a quick check under all the desks reveals nothing, so you head to the Fitz next. The Fitz might be your favorite telescope, despite the rickety wheeled ladder you have to balance on precariously to look through it. You check around the room in all the nooks and crannies where you usually set things when you need your hands free for a moment, but all you find is someone's textbook. You're about to leave when you realize you should check the ladder itself; you've definitely used it as a shelf before. Alas, there is nothing on the ladder, either.

You go back to the Orange to check on Sophie, unsure of how long you've been searching. You open the door into darkness.

"Hello?" you call into the void, hand reaching along the wall for the light switch. "Sophie? What happened?"

You find the switch and flip it, blinking as your eyes adjust, then blinking at what you see. The room is empty.

"What the *fuck*," you say, heart beating a mile a minute. You run back to the classroom to see if maybe she's there, which she isn't, and then you check the Fitz even though you were just there. You run back to the Orange when you don't find her; the lower room is still empty, but you didn't check upstairs. Maybe she didn't hear you call?

The upper portion of the Orange is still lit, though you thought you'd turned the lights off. Sophie isn't there, but the phone you found is, the one that died. Had you given that to her to hold? You don't remember.

You cross the room to the phone and go to pick it up, but freeze. You blink. You take a deep breath through your nose and let it out through your mouth and squeeze your eyes shut for a count of three before opening them again. What you see hasn't changed.

There, propped against the dome of the Orange telescope, is an older iPhone, just one sticker on its heavy-duty purple case. You pick it up, turn it on. The time 1:20 glows white against the dark hair of an anime character you *do* recognize.

This is your phone.

You turn it off and put it back on the shelf, look around the room. No other phones to be seen. You go back downstairs and scour that room for the other phone, but it's not there, and neither is Sophie. You sit on the stairs and consider the likelihood that you've lost your mind. You think you might scream, just to release some tension. You don't; instead, you go back upstairs and retrieve your phone. You put it in your pocket with suspicion, keep a hand on it just in case, then go to look at the hatch cover for the staircase.

It looks the same as it always does, not dented at all from any impacts, no sign of blood. Just black painted wood, heavy and unwieldy. You turn off the upstairs lights and descend slowly, then carefully pull the hatch down over your head. The underside has no marks, either. You take one last look around the downstairs room of the Orange telescope, see nothing untoward, nothing out of place, no sign of Sophie at all, not even blood on the floor, which strikes you as odd given how much she was bleeding. You reconsider screaming but decide not to again. You don't know what might be listening.

You go from telescope building to telescope building, checking each one, then locking it after you, even the Alden, which the class hadn't used. You check the classroom building last, and it's empty, too. There's no blood on the snow outside, no trail of footprints to follow. How does a person vanish into thin air? You don't want to think about it, but you have to. Best case scenario, Sophie wasn't hurt as badly as you thought and has just made her way back to her dorm without saying goodbye. Worst case scenario, you're losing your mind. In-between scenario, perhaps stress can cause hallucinations. It *is* almost finals, and you *are* behind in your reading for two classes. There are maybe some other options, but you *really* don't want to think about them.

You take one last circuit around the observatory; everything is locked and dark, and there's no sign of Sophie. You take your phone out of your pocket; it's still your phone. What else is there to do? You leave.

You're halfway to your dorm when your phone goes off. You silence it immediately but hesitate to pull it out, dread knotting itself up in your chest, threatening to choke you. You stand there for what might be thirty seconds or five minutes, the cold forgotten, but in the end it's not really a choice. You pull out your phone and look. There's a text notification on your lock screen from an unknown number. The message just says, "Thanks."

The Brick, built in 1858.

A fire destroyed the third and four floors in 1932; only the third floor has been restored.

BLACK BOX
JULIANA GRAY

THREE WEEKS, AND the professor still hadn't learned to unmute herself at the beginning of class. Miri turned back to the first page of her notebook and added a slash to the tally she kept there. The faces in tight rows on her screen stayed carefully blank as Dr. White waved and mouthed at them. Finally, her lips formed an "oh", and she leaned toward her keyboard.

"There we go! Good morning!" her voice chirped through Miri's earbuds. She unmuted herself, called "Good morning," and immediately hit mute again. There, she'd participated. She opened a new tab in Canvas while Dr. White called roll; once the lecture started, she could work on her response assignment for Global Studies.

"Let's see, Ryan's here, Miriam's here," Dr. White said.

Miri gave a little wave at the camera. Class participation was worth 10% of the course grade.

"Ahmad is here, or at least his box is here. Ahmad, are you with us? Could you say something?"

There was an agonizing pause of perhaps five seconds, and then a sleepy voice said, "Yeah, I'm here."

"Great. And Catherine, are you with us?" More silence. Catherine was one of the black boxes; Dr. White "strongly encouraged" students to turn on their cameras, but didn't require it, so only about half of the class showed their faces. Some turned them on at the beginning and then went dark, and some never activated them at all. Catherine was one of those: no photo, no last name, just "catie" on a small rectangle.

"Catherine? Catie?" Dr. White called.

Finally, a small voice whispered, "I'm here."

"Okay, thank you." Dr. White moved through the rest of the roll, saying something about how Banner still didn't seem to be accurate or have the right names, so students should email her if she was missing their names or getting them wrong. Miri tilted her screen so that only the top of her head showed on camera and bent to her Global Studies assignment.

She looked up again about twenty minutes later, realizing that Dr. White had asked a question.

"Could you give me a wave or use the little response thing if you live in the Brick?" the professor repeated. Miri clicked the button and a tiny yellow hand appeared in her box. A few other hands appeared: Makenzie, Alex, Paul, Catie. She had no idea who these people were. She'd been isolated in her single room, seeing almost no one but a few friends from the softball team, since mid-August.

"The Brick was used as a barracks during the first World War, and when the 1918 influenza epidemic hit, part of the building was used as an infirmary," Dr. White was saying. "I know you think COVID is bad, and of course it is, but the 1918 flu was just devastating. Five Alfred students and two teachers died."

Miri blinked. This was actually interesting. Where in the Brick, she wondered?

Which floor? Probably the basement; that would be the easiest place to get sick people in and out of. Miri's room was on the third floor, so probably not one where somebody had died. Probably.

"Alex, I see in the chat that you've called it the Spanish flu," Dr. White said. "It was called that at the time, but the flu didn't originate in Spain, and that name was used partly to minimize the danger in the American press. The Spanish actually called it the French flu."

Miri snorted. Alex was another black box, a mansplainer—womansplainer? nonbinarysplainer? she didn't know—who loved to pop into the chat with comments and corrections but never spoke a word.

"Smackdown," she whispered at the screen.

Suddenly, a sharp yowl like an angry cat hissed through her earbuds. The rows of faces flinched, hands reaching for their volume controls. Miri pulled out her earbuds and scanned the boxes. There, outlined in yellow: "catie."

"Good morning!" Dr. White called after she finally unmuted herself. Miri mouthed the words back but didn't bother to unmute. She'd been up all night texting with her little brother. Sammy was still in high school back in Rochester, but without football, he had zero motivation to do any work for his classes and was in danger of flunking out. Their mom was a nurse at Strong Hospital, and Sammy spent most of his energy worrying about her. Miri tried to give him pep talks, but it was hard, since she didn't have any motivation either. Why should they get up and stare at these screens when they weren't

learning anything anyway? What kind of job could she get after she graduated, if the world was still in lockdown? Honestly, why fucking bother?

"Catherine, are you there?" Dr. White asked. The same thing, every day.

A chat box popped up. It was Alex. "Catie is sick," it said.

"Catherine? Catie?" Dr. White called. "Are you there? Are you not feeling well?"

A fizzing noise, then that small voice. "I'm here."

"Are you feeling all right? Alex says you're ill."

That fizz, like damp static. Then, "I'm here. I'm cold."

Miri looked out her open window at the blue September sky and maple branches thick with green leaves. Cold? It was probably 65 out there. She was already warm in her hoodie.

"Do you have chills?" Dr. White was asking. "Did you do the daily screening?"

Hiss, fizz. "Sorry, my WiFi's having problems. I have to go." Catie's black box disappeared.

"It is terrible in the Brick," Alex typed in the chat.

"Yeah, it's bad," Paul chimed in.

Dr. White sighed. "Okay. Let's talk about the midterm."

Miri slammed the door behind her, threw her mask on the bed and opened her laptop. She was late; she'd used the app to place her Starbucks order in plenty of time, but there was only one poor guy working there and the line was long. Now she sipped her strawberry frappe as she opened Canvas and found the Zoom link.

She needn't have rushed; Dr. White was telling a story about her cat. The animal in question, a fat calico, perched on a bookshelf behind the professor, contentedly licking her own butt. Still, Miri turned on her camera and smiled so the professor could see she was happy to be there.

The frappuccino was too sweet, soggy strawberries bobbing like corpses in the creamy froth. Today was Wednesday, Humpday, Slumpday; she'd needed something to cheer herself up and had hoped to run into someone she knew in Powell. But it was hard to recognize people in masks, and no one would meet her eyes as they stood six feet away. Now she was back in her room, her mouth aching with sugar, alone and staring at a screen again.

Her phone buzzed. Sammy had sent her a TikTok of some guys dancing to "Blinding Lights."

"Ur supposed to be in class," she texted.

A pause, then three pulsing dots. "So r u."

"Some of you haven't yet posted your essay topic in the Canvas discussion," Dr. White was saying. "Ahmad, Kayleigh, Alex, Catherine, could you tell me what you're planning to write your essay about?"

Miri had a flash of panic, then remembered that she had posted an essay topic about Woodrow Wilson being a tremendous racist. Dr. White had seemed to like that.

When was the essay due?

"Okay, Ahmad, so you're going to get back to me," Dr. White said. "Kayleigh, Alex, Catherine, what about you?"

In the chat, Alex wrote, "Theodore Roosevelt was the greatest American president. He built the Panama Canal and ended the Russo Japanese War."

Dr. White frowned, leaning closer to her screen. "Okay, Alex, I see you've posted about Roosevelt in the chat, but that's a pretty broad topic. You and I should make an appointment to see if we can narrow it down and come up with a thesis. Okay?"

Silence. The calico had finished ministering to its butt and fallen asleep.

"Catherine, what are you planning to write about?" Catie's black box at the bottom of the screen remained inert. Dr. White spoke louder. "Catherine? Catie? Are you with us?"

A yellow bar beneath the black box flickered to life. "Yeah," said a tiny voice. It sounded drained, distant, like she was speaking from the moon. "I'm here."

"Okay, great. Do you have a topic yet for your midterm essay?"

A hiss like a lunar wind, then a whisper. "I don't know."

Dr. White made a frustrated noise in her throat. "Well, you need to figure it out soon. You and Ahmad and the other students who missed the deadline to post, you need to—"

"I don't know if I should even *be* here," wailed the small voice. Catie's black box stayed outlined in yellow as the earbuds emitted sounds that might be sobs.

From somewhere in the building Miri heard a crash, and the lamp above her bed went out. Not just the lamp – the overhead light clicked dark, and her minifridge ceased its constant hum. From next door Miri heard a muffled voice ask, "What the fuck?"

Miri's laptop battery was fully charged, and Dr. White was still talking. "Catie, I don't mean to upset you, but –" The screen flared white for a millisecond, then blacked out.

"Oh shit," Miri muttered and tapped some keys, trying to bring the machine back to life. Finally, it restarted, but the Wi-Fi was out.

"Fuck," Miri said. Outside she heard doors opening, people talking. She slipped the loops of her mask over her ears and stepped into the hall. It was probably ten degrees colder out here, and she shivered under the dim emergency lights. Almost every door on her hall was open, masked faces leaning out.

"You think it's just us, or the whole university?" asked a guy with chocolate brown eyes over a blue mask.

"I don't know," Miri said. "I was in class, and my Zoom like, exploded."

The guy pointed at her. "Wait. Dr. White's class?"

Miri nodded.

"I thought I recognized you!" the guy said. "I'm Paul. I usually don't turn on my camera."

"Oh, hey," Miri said. She felt self-conscious, suddenly horribly aware that she'd been wearing the same leggings and hoodie for almost a week. "That's so random."

"Right?" Paul said. "Well, I guess classes are cancelled."

"Yeah, I guess so," Miri said. "Hey, do you know if that girl Catie lives in this building?"

He rolled his eyes. "There are probably ten girls named Catie in The Brick."

Miri looked up and down the hall, trying to read the faces. "Yeah, I guess so." She nodded at the guy, returned to her room and locked the door behind her.

The power and Wi-Fi had been restored almost immediately, so by the time Miri logged back into class on Friday she'd almost forgotten the whole thing. But as soon as she was admitted to the Zoom her ears were hit by that awful hiss. She yanked out her earbuds and turned the laptop speakers way down.

Dr. White was clicking at something on her keyboard while students shouted over the noise or wrote in the chat, trying to tell her what she needed to do to mute the students. Several people in the class were absent, and those who were in attendance almost all had their cameras off. Miri's screen showed row upon row of black boxes, neatly lined up like coffins. One black box—Catie's—was outlined in yellow, screeching.

Then the screen went silent.

Dr. White leaned forward, her eyes scanning the screen. "Okay! Whew!" she said. "It sounds like we're still having some technical difficulties. Catherine, is there an audio problem on your end? Something wrong with your microphone? You can type it in the chat."

Instead of Catie's words, Alex's appeared. "Catie is sick. She needs help."

"Catie, are you all right?" Dr. White asked. "Alex, are you with her?"

"I am with Catie," Alex wrote. "Catie needs help. Please help."

Miri stood up instinctively but sat down again. What could she do? Why should she do anything? This girl was supposedly in the Brick, but she didn't know where. Or Alex might just be pulling a prank.

"Catie?" Dr. White asked. "Catie, are you –"

The noise came whooshing back at full volume like a cave full of angry bats. Miri could barely hear Dr. White's cry of "it says everyone's muted!" over the roar.

"Catie needs help," Alex wrote. "She is in the Brick. Second floor. West end. Please help. Catie is sick. Please help."

Miri sucked in a breath. "Fuck it." She stood, pulled on her mask and ran into the hall. It was freezing. She ran to the stairs and down to the second floor. Which way was west? She pictured the sunset falling over the hills on the other side of Main Street and sprinted in that direction.

She could hear the hissing noise, now coming from somewhere within the Brick, growing louder as she ran. In life, unmitigated by broadband and tinny speakers, the noise was more like a moan, like a mother bear keening over a drowned cub. Miri stopped in front of a door decorated with a cheerful cardboard sign that said RA and banged on it with her fist.

"Hey, a girl on this floor needs help!" she yelled. "Hey! This is a fucking emergency!"

A low voice came through the door. "Just a minute!"

"Get off your ass and get out here!" Miri shouted. She waited a second longer, then took off down the hallway again.

There were no names on the doors, but she knew she'd found Catie's, the next-to-last door on the right, by the yowling coming from the other side. Miri knocked.

"Catie? Is that you? Are you okay?" If there was any sound from inside, she couldn't hear it over the moan. Miri touched the knob and jerked her hand back; it burned cold like dry ice. She pulled her sleeve over her hand and tried again, but the knob was locked. "Catie? Are you all right? Can you let me in?"

A tall guy in basketball shorts and a paper mask – he must be the RA—ran to Miri's side. "What's going on? What's that noise?" he asked.

"The girl that lives here is sick. She needs help, but the door's locked." Miri jiggled the knob again.

The guy frowned. "Are you sure? Did she call you, or—"

Miri whipped around. The RA was at least six inches taller than she was, but she stared him down the way her tiny mother did Sammy whenever he was being an idiot. "This girl needs help *now*. You have keys to these rooms, right?"

"Yeah, but—"

"Then go get them!"

The RA hesitated, bouncing on his feet, then took off back down the hall towards his room.

By now a couple of other doors on the hall had opened, people drawn by Miri's shouts and the weird sound emanating from behind the locked door.

"Somebody call 911!" Miri yelled. She jerked the frigid doorknob again. She wanted to kick the door down, but she knew that only worked in movies. "Come on, open up, open up, open—"

A gush of air like an arctic wind blasted the door open. The room was a wreck, clothes and papers strewn on the floor, old food containers piled atop the mini-fridge and desk. On the bed next to an open laptop was a person. And something . . . else.

Miri stepped closer. The whooshing, moaning wind blew her hair into her face, but she could see a girl dressed in sweatpants and a hoodie lying on the sheets, the rest of the bedclothes pushed to the side as if they'd been flung off her. Hovering over the unmoving girl was a vague shape like a broad smear of silver paint. It seemed to gather itself inches above the bed, before streaming into Catie's open mouth and nose. A few seconds later, it rushed out, thinner, less *there*, then gathered itself again.

"Catie?" Miri said. "Catie, are you okay? What is that. . . that thing? Catie?" She took another step closer but was afraid to touch the pale form. Catie's lips and eyelids were blue. "Catie?"

The laptop buzzed and spun itself around so that Miri could see the screen. It was open, absurdly, to their Zoom class. There was Dr. White in her tiny box, babbling silently. In the chat, words spun up and up. "Catie needs help. Catie is sick. Please help Catie. The Brick, second floor. Help Catie." All from Alex.

Miri's eyes lifted from the chat to the shimmering silver cloud exhaling from Catie's body. "Alex?"

The laptop buzzed as if its parts were grinding themselves to dust. "Help Catie," Alex said in the chat. "I am breathing for her. But her heart. I cannot."

Shivering, Miri reached out her hand. It passed through the edge of the silver blur, and Miri felt a cold tingle in her fingertips. She touched Catie's cool neck, searching for a pulse. She found nothing.

"She needs CPR," she yelled over the wind. Was she talking to a fucking cloud? A ghost? Evidently, she was. "I need to give her chest compressions."

The cloud shifted, making room for Miri at the bedside. She pressed the heel of her right hand over Catie's chest, placed her left hand atop her right, and twined her fingers together. The silvery haze floated beside her head; she could sense it waiting. Miri drew in a deep breath and pushed. "One. Two. Three. Four."

She pumped to a count of thirty and paused. "Your turn," she said to the cloud. Firmly but gently, it flowed into Catie's mouth and nose, and Miri saw her chest rise. It exhaled, now so faint it was barely detectable. "Again," she ordered. The cloud swirled, cohered, and flowed into Catie again, then out. Miri placed her folded hands over Catie's heart and pressed.

How long did they work together, girl and ghost? Miri wasn't sure. Suddenly there was a clattering of stretchers and equipment, and an EMT gently pushed Miri aside, telling her she could stop. As they fitted an oxygen mask over Catie's face, a pale silver tendril unspooled from her lips, floated to the ceiling and vanished. Miri found herself in a crowd of gawking students and realized the condensation in her face mask had frozen solid.

Later, she heard rumors that Catie had swallowed all of her anti-depression and anti-anxiety meds; she also heard that Catie was diabetic and hadn't been eating; she also heard that Catie's appendix had burst; she also heard that Catie had gotten food poisoning from a turkey wrap at Ade. Later, Dr. White told the class that Catie had made a full recovery and taken a medical leave of absence; she never mentioned Alex, and his black box did not return to their class. Later, Paul told her that he'd been one of the students watching her perform the chest compressions, and that she'd looked like a superhero. Later, Paul, he of the beautiful chocolate-brown eyes, would tell her a lot of things, wonderful things, but he never mentioned seeing a silver cloud, and she never asked.

Now, in the Brick, as the RA scolded her for breaking the lock, Miri rolled her aching shoulders. She was cold and exhausted, and her hands and face were numb, but she felt better than she had in weeks. She walked past the RA, past the knot of masked students lingering in the hall. She ripped off her mask as she descended the stairs and plunged through the door into the late autumn sun. She felt alive.

Nightmare On Park Street

Robert Giancarlo

WHAT I AM about to tell you on this paper has lived rent free in my head for the past 10 years. Whenever I share this story with someone, they shrug it off as mere nonsense and superstition, and no one more than my therapist. She has this idea that if I write down all my thoughts on these events, she may be able to deconstruct them and release my mind from the clutches of what happened that insane night. But I swear on my grandfather's grave, these are factual events.

It was a typical freezing November night in Alfred. Finals were quickly approaching, and I wished I was back home in sunny Florida to bring some positive closure to that damned year. Of course, I speak of the year 2020, a year where a pandemic shut everything down and robbed me of my final year of the college experience. I wished to be back home so badly, partying in the nice weather, not giving the mask or social distancing stuff any thought. Yeah, I know that sounds selfish, but I paid a lot of money to come to Alfred, and nobody can blame me for being pissed that I couldn't get the full experience!

Out of spite for my crappy situation, I decided that I was going to invite the boys over to my dorm in the Brick to get drunk. Turn on a sports game, blast the music, and just get friggin' wasted was my plan. I had some Captain Morgan left, but only, like, two drinks worth. Also, I was out of Coke. So I knocked down the two shots and prepared to go get more rum and Coke at the liquor store.

As I left, a gust of wind came through my open window. Even though Alfred is cold, living in the Brick means you have to leave your window open at all times or the room will be over 80 degrees, thanks to the outdated heating system. The wind seemed to be speaking to me. In a low, miserable voice, I swear I heard someone moan, "Let me out."

I gasped. What the hell was that? I must be imagining things.

As I was walking through the hallway, something about the building just gave off creepy vibes. The way the lights flickered that night reminded me of an abandoned asylum. It took me back to the mental hospital themed haunted houses, another thing that coronavirus took away from me that year.

Earlier in the semester, my biology class had talked about the history of the Brick. It had been a Civil War infirmary, the kind where gravely wounded soldiers would be given whiskey to nullify the oncoming pain of amputation. Coincidentally, this ratchety old building had also held poor souls suffering from influenza, a pandemic from a century before the one going on now.

The walk to the liquor store felt like an eternity. It was even darker than usual outside because a couple of the street lights were dead. No matter how hard I tried, I couldn't get what I had heard out of my head. Normally, the liquor would have made negativity ebb away, but this time, I couldn't stop thinking about the voice. I had heard of spirits possibly wandering around Alfred from buddies of mine in the suites whose doors would open and close randomly in the middle of the night, and on top of that, there was all the awful stuff that went on in the Brick.

Apparently, people could tell that something about me seemed off that night. When I got to the liquor store, the owner asked, "Son, what's wrong? You look like you've seen a ghost."

I shuddered. "I'm fine, Fred. Everything is all good in this neighborhood."

Deep down, I knew I was lying. I knew there was something very troubling going on in this neighborhood but I couldn't put my damn finger on what was happening.

The freezing trek back from the store only made my night worse. As I got closer to my dorm, the wind began to pick up. I crossed the bridge over Canacadea Creek while it howled like crazy, and that's when I saw it. One of the many deer that hung out in the woods behind the Brick was shaking, rocking back and forth violently. The poor thing was having a seizure.

"What the fuck?" I stared in shock. "I didn't know deer could be epileptic." The poor buck looked as if it had been possessed by a devil. It shook uncontrollably, unable to break free from the painful convulsions.

I stood there, trying to plan my next move. Should I call public safety? The cops? I was only 20 at the time, so these options were definitely off limits with this handle of rum in my hand. I thought about calling animal control, but it was pretty late, and something about the deer just made me freeze.

I didn't notice it at first, but something was wrong with this alpha deer's eyes. Initially, I was too nervous to approach the ailing buck; eventually, something told me to help him out, literally.

"Come closer," said the deer.

It was the same voice from my room earlier. I almost pissed my pants.

Slowly, even though I was shaking, I crept towards this poor animal. Then, with yellow eyes resembling that of a demon, the deer said, "You're next."

I shrieked. Fight or flight kicked in, and I was in no position to fight this possessed animal. I clutched my bottles of rum and Coke like I was Derrick Henry and sprinted across the bridge, up the hill, and finally back to my room at the top of the Brick.

Damn, I was out of breath when I got back to my room. Vaping and not being able to use the gym with any regularity, thanks to COVID, definitely didn't help. The funny thing is that I almost blacked out during the run. I remember how I got back to my room, but while I was running, it was as if my mind turned off and my only goal was to get to safety. My body was literally on autopilot.

I grabbed my shot glass out of my closet and started pounding the booze. I think I had, like, four or five shots in 10 minutes. Then I remembered that I had a night to enjoy. For now, the liquor had worked things out. Being a Florida man, there is nothing I am more passionate about than Florida Gators football. I turned on the game, which was against rival Georgia, five minutes before kickoff.

"Ahhh, yes," I said contentedly. "Time to invite the boys over."

Since the game was about to start, I told them to drive over. Being somewhat responsible, I offered up my room as a spot where they could crash for the night, rather than crash their car on some back road later on.

I heard them sprinting up the stairs just as the Gators lined up to kick off. "Hurry your asses up!" I called.

One would think that after all the hullabaloo I would have locked my door, but I didn't. They all broke in like the SWAT team except for my buddy Bob, the designated driver, who wandered in more calmly. We were a dumb bunch, but we weren't dumb enough to drink and drive—though it looked like some of the boys had already started drinking.

Being the only currently sober friend, Bob actually had his wits about him. When I went to high five him, Bob yelled, "Hey, what the hell, man?"

"What's wrong, dude?"

"There's blood pouring down your arm, all over your shirt, and now all over me, you dumbass!"

I looked and found that I had a huge open wound on my elbow. I must have been too drunk to notice.

"How wasted are you, man? There was blood on the front door when we got here and it was dripping all the way down the hallway to your room. How could you not have noticed?"

"Damn, must've cut it while I was running."

"What were you running from, the fucking bogeyman?"

I gulped. "Nothing, man, I'm just drunk."

I wasn't about to tell them the truth. They would've called me a puss, said I was crazy, or both. Kind of like anyone who hears this story. But I don't care. This story is as true as death.

I waited until the commercial break to clean my cut. A true Florida man goes through any pain to see his team play. I grabbed some band aids and rubbing alcohol, then stumbled down the hallway to the bathroom.

The bathroom was freezing cold; some idiot left the window open. Well, I guess I couldn't blame them. As I said, the Brick's heating system could roast anybody, even in the dead of Alfred winter.

The wind went nuts as I began to clean my battle wound. Moments later, the lights flickered, and the hand dryer started going on and off.

"Something ain't right," I thought to myself. "This better not be more spiritual bullshit."

Bang! One of the stall doors slammed shut. I looked back; there was nobody in there or in any of the other stalls. I didn't want to be a creep, but I was getting real nervous now, so I went back and checked the showers; still no sign of anybody.

"Okay," I said. "Time to chill the fuck out for a second."

I took a couple deep breaths to get my drunken wits about me. I rolled up my sleeve to start washing the cut. After I cleared out the blood, the wind began to blow again, and I swear it mumbled something. Don't forget, I was drunk, but I wasn't deaf.

The wind groaned, "Hello there, my friend."

"Shit! What do you want from me?"

I looked in the mirror. I promise that this is not fiction. Yes, I was drunk as hell, but I swear that I saw this.

Staring back at me was a man, his skin as green as a witch. He was around my age, but looked wretched. I swear on my grandfather's grave that I saw him. He looked like a college kid, but a sickly and maimed one. The spirit had the outline of a human, except he was missing one of his forearms.

"Come with me," he muttered.

"Argh!"

I had never been so scared in my life. First, I had demon deer threatening me and now an actual ghost? I didn't know what to make of it. To be honest, I still don't really know what to make of it. None of that matters, though. The ghost was there; I saw him with my own two eyes.

Of course, I took off screaming. I didn't even finish bandaging up the cut. I just sprinted out of the bathroom like Usain Bolt.

I got back to the room in what felt like nanoseconds. My buddies were all laughing their heads off when I got there. Had they seen what I had seen, they sure as hell wouldn't have been laughing.

"Bro, what are you, five?" blubbered Lucas. "Did Dracula come out and try to kill you, ya little bitch? Is Casper the ghost after you, ya goon?"

I couldn't take hiding it anymore. "I swear, man, I saw a damn ghost," I snapped. "I don't know what's going on here or what the fuck is living in this building, but something here is straight up shot."

Lucas only laughed harder. "How much have you been drinking man? You sure you didn't put the wrong kind of mushrooms on your pizza earlier, dude? If so, let me get some, brother!"

"Whatever, man, but I swear on my life that some supernatural bastard is living here and is trying to kill me!"

"Why don't you have another drink, you moron?" Bob said.

"Fuck it, man, I gotta get right. Give me the damn bottle." I popped the cap and just chugged it down. I was so stressed out I didn't even bother to pour a shot.

That made me feel better. "Finally," I thought, turning back to the game on TV. "This craziness is starting to fade." The Florida Georgia game is like a civil war where I'm from, and we were winning before the half. Being my drunk self, I was going nuts, screaming like a banshee at any mildly good play made by my Gator squad. My buddies weren't Florida fans, so they didn't care all that much, but believe me, I was going crazy.

When halftime came, I took my usual bathroom break.

"Are you gonna cry like a little bitch again?" laughed Paul.

"Fuck off, dude, just let me piss in peace." And that's what I did. For whatever reason, I didn't get attacked by a spirit when I went to the bathroom. I was relieved. "The worst is behind me," I thought. "The insanity has finally left me."

I washed my hands, left the bathroom and walked back to my dorm safely. Sound normal? Well, it sure as hell didn't seem that way on that night. After what had happened earlier, I wondered if the entire world would collapse.

Bob instantly asked, "Was Hannibal Lecter following you around the bathroom?"

"Real funny, jackass," I said.

I finally started to really enjoy myself. My Gators were kicking some Georgia Bulldog ass, and by the time the third quarter ended, we were up three TDs. I was so wasted that I incessantly did the Gator chomp with my arms.

"This is why you don't bet against my Gators!" I yelled to Bob. Poor guy put $100 on Georgia to win and didn't get a cent of that money back.

"Shut the hell up, man."

Then the power went out, plunging us into darkness.

"What the fuck?!" I screamed, slurring my words. "Yo, this game ain't over yet! I gotta see this!" We all were fuming. It was a typical 2020 thing: something good was happening, and then it all became miserable.

"Damn, why does this year have to suck so badly?" Bob grumbled.

A loud gust of wind swept through the room.

"It's only going to get worse for you."

"What the hell?" I whirled around in the dark. "Did you guys just say something?"

Replies of "Nah, bro," echoed back.

"Then who said that?"

I looked around the room to see if it was this spirit guy again. My phone flashlight revealed my finished bottle of Malibu lying capless on the ground.

"Yup," said the voice. "I'm about to make this year a lot more miserable for you, buddy."

"Why are you doing this to me?" I yelled. "What have I ever done to you? Why me? What on earth do you even want?"

"We've been waiting for 100 years to find a new companion. We're gonna show you what we went through: a bloody war and a disgusting pandemic."

"Leave me alone man. I don't want to die!"

And then, the same horrible spirit I saw in the mirror came flying out of the Malibu bottle, growing to life-size as he did. This time he had brought friends, and they swirled around the room. I could tell by the voice that one of them was the monster who possessed the deer earlier. They all looked sick and had at least one limb amputated. I didn't know what to think. I just started screaming at the top of my lungs, not giving a damn if my friends or anyone else in the building heard. I was scared shitless.

One of the spirits declared, "Don't worry. This will be extremely painful!" Then, they all came rushing at me, tugging me toward the bottle. I held onto my bedpost for dear life.

"Where are you taking me?" I screamed.

"We've been stuck in this miserable building for a century, tortured by boredom, unable to escape," said one of them cheerily. "We just want to make things a little more interesting, that's all!"

"Get the fuck away from me! I won't let you take me alive!" I gripped my bedpost, but it felt hopeless. I was like a crumb being sucked into a vacuum of torment. Just before they pulled me into the bottle, I blacked out.

I woke up the next morning at St. James Hospital in Hornell. They had to pump my stomach to get rid of all the booze. I had never felt more hungover in my entire life, but at least Bob was there to keep me company. More importantly, I was alive, and I had survived the attack.

"What happened last night, bro?" Bob asked when I finally woke up.

I thought about telling him, but I figured I'd better wait. I had finals to study for, and I didn't want to be studying in the looney bin.

A couple months later, I told my buddies who were there that night the truth. They didn't believe me, and neither did anyone who wasn't there. I can't force anyone to believe this story, but just be careful around the Brick at Alfred University. Something ain't right about that place!

ANOTHER BRICK IN THE WALL

NOAH T. HOWARD

"WHAT DID I do to land myself here, you ask?" I laughed. "Nothing that merits being confined to this place with the likes of you. Too bad the judge didn't agree." I stopped talking for a moment and scanned my new room for the hundredth time since arriving yesterday. Brick walls, a toilet that doubles as a sink, and two beds that aren't much softer than the walls. I smiled. "Well, you've told me your story, so let me tell you mine. Just don't get jealous that you weren't chosen, like me."

For weeks—months, maybe—I'd heard these strange noises and seen these strange sights. It was always around the Witching Hour, but I didn't believe in that garbage. As a pre-med student, nothing bothered me except for real issues with the human body. I guess that's also why I always stayed up so late studying for my exams. That's when it was the most quiet, and I never had been able to ignore distractions.

Everyone told me that "The Brick" was haunted and that it used to be some old Civil War hospital or something. It was an old brick residence hall, hence its name. The interior supported creaking wooden floors that looked like they'd been there for a thousand years. I'd heard that students experienced unsettling things, which evidently wasn't uncommon. They say soldiers spent their last minutes in agony within those halls.

33

Maybe that's true, or maybe my friends just liked trying to scare me into some sleepless nights. Either way, my roommate thought I was crazy. That's what he said, but he always slept through those noises and whatever the hell else I saw.

"You're bonkers, Blake," he'd groan to me. "There's literally nothing there. Just go to bed already; it's practically [insert whatever ungodly hour here]."

I didn't care what he said. With the residence hall being as old as it was, I was sure there had to be a simple scientific explanation for the noises. As for the sights, the phenomenon was no different than when you stay at a friend's house for the first time. I just hadn't become used to sleeping there yet, was all.

Crack.

"What was that?" I thought.

"Hey! Psst. Jeremy, wake up!" I threw my shoe at my roommate, but he didn't stir, as usual. One second he was awake, and the next he'd be out. I knew he heard it. He had to; our room wasn't very big. It only contained enough space for each of us to have a desk, a dresser, a small and uncomfortable bed, and a makeshift closet. Nestled between the closets, on the far side of the room, sat our window.

No matter what, Jeremy always passed out right before the phenomena started to happen. I felt bad sometimes; I would force him to stay up so the episodes didn't start, but I'd never admit that to him.

I sighed and went back to my studies. I'd be damned if I was going to let the "heebie-jeebies" make me fail my upcoming test. Still, I couldn't shake this feeling like something was in the room with me. I looked around, wondering what the cause of the noises could be. The dark, lonely room offered no solution. The shadows danced on the walls. But whose shadows were they? The only light in the room appeared to be the dim glow from my desk lamp, and not a thing moved.

I could feel the blood rushing through my ears. My heart beat so loudly, I was sure it would be the one thing that could wake Jeremy. What was the source of these awful noises? Cracks, pops, and just about every possible sound-effect echoed within the confines of my dorm room. The more I tried to ignore them, the louder and more frequent they became.

Crack. Tap. Scratch.

My palms grew sweaty. "What the *hell* is that?!" I stood up, and my chair squeaked across the floor. *Huuuunkchooooo.* What was making that noise? *Tap. Scratch.* The window. Something was tapping the window! I ran over and threw it open. The torn screen allowed half of my body to lean out as I looked down all... three... stories. Who the hell could knock on a window three stories up? That simply wasn't possible. Was it? The chill of the wind clawed at me. It whistled in my ears, taunting me. In the darkness, I could see nothing but a few shadows making their way around the grassy fields of Alfred. A strange feeling came over me once more. I felt a presence behind me, the stale air brushing against my skin.

Huuuuuunkchooooooo.

Terrified, I let out a yell and jumped back into the room, slamming the window shut. During the commotion, the 'hunkchoo' seemed to have paused, though I was sure that something was there. My eyes fell on the shoe I had thrown moments before. It lay right beside Jeremy's bed. Was that where it landed? Wasn't it on its side, not right-side-up? I was certain it had been moved. I sprinted over and knelt beside it, picking it up. I examined it for a second, turning it over. It seemed normal; no ectoplasm dripped from it. That's what ghosts do, right? They leave ectoplasm everywhere. Well, there wasn't any on the shoe anyway, but I was sure it moved from where I last saw it and I knew damn well Jeremy couldn't have been the one to touch it.

Without warning, a tight grip seized my shoulder and whirled me around. I threw the shoe instinctively as I turned, letting out a war cry. I wasn't going down without a fight. The demon or ghost or whatever it was that wanted to kill me was going to have a hell of a time trying. The shoe connected with the wall just inches above Jeremy's head, who was standing behind me, and fell inanimately to the ground once more. It was then that I realized the 'hunkchoo' had been coming from Jeremy's windpipe. That son of a bitch never could stop snoring.

"What is your problem?!" he asked me. "It's two in the morning and you're screaming and sprinting around the room like a dog that's got to take a piss. Do you need to go to the Wellness Center or something? You're losing it, man."

"You're awake! You heard that right? Right...?" I must have looked at him like he had two heads. "Jeremy, please tell me you heard that shit! The noises, the window!"

Now came his turn to look at me as though I was the nut-job. "Blake, you need to stop staying up so late. This place ain't haunted, and the people that say it is are just tryna scare you, bro. The noise outside the window was probably the tree. Go to bed and put that damn book away. Maybe that's what's driving you insane." He climbed back into bed, rolled over and instantly began snoozing once more.

I shook off the feeling I had and decided that, perhaps, the best course of action would be to splash some cold water on my face. If it worked in the movies, it could work for me. I raced through the creaking hallways, the floors groaning under my weight. I burst through the bathroom door; it made a loud smack against the wall. Inside, I found four lonely stalls accompanied by a couple of sinks and two urinals: the floor damp, the mirrors foggy, and the urinals unflushed. The sink squeaked and resisted my pull, but eventually submitted. The cold water stung my cheeks.

I looked in the mirror and rubbed my eyes. This was it. I was finally losing it. There's no such thing as the paranormal; I was just tired, that was all. That's right. I just needed more sleep. It had to be because I drank too much caffeine, maybe. Right? That could be the only solution. I just needed—*Bop. Dun. Dun-Dun.*

The man in the mirror stared back at me. After a brief moment, his brown eyes grew wide, showing the string-like veins in them. He turned around slowly, one fist clenched and ready for action. Only, nothing was there. I was alone in the bathroom. Or was I? I heard more noise coming from one of the stalls. I finally got the ghost. I could catch it and be done. As long as it didn't fade through the wall or whatever it is that those sons of bitches do.

I began at the stall to the far left, kicking it open. Nothing. "Janet," I yelled like a game show host, "What's behind door number two?!" I kicked the next one open. "Show 'em what we have in door number three!" The next stall opened just as easily. The fourth and final stall stood, daring me to touch it. This was sure to be the one. There had to be something in that bathroom with me. I was positive. I held my breath for a second and thought. The first three stalls were empty, and this was the only one left. I heard a shuffling noise within. I smiled.

"We wouldn't want our contestant to go home empty-handed, now would we?!" I kicked it, but it wouldn't budge. I kicked it again and again. "Janet! Give. Me. The. Damn. Prize!" I pounded on the door and shook it back and forth.

"Bro, what the hell?!" The ghost was talking to me, wasn't it? It was cursing me out and screaming. I heard it fidgeting around and, against my hands, felt it shaking the whole stall. It sounded as if the whole structure was going to collapse. It was trying to kill me! It taunted me, saying the same things Jeremy would say. "What is wrong with you? You're crazy!"

But it wasn't a ghost at all. It was some poor kid trying to empty his bowels. I sunk my head in defeat. "My bad, man." I ignored his following remarks as I headed back to my room. As I walked through the creaky hallways, I couldn't help but notice the bricks. The goddamn bricks were looking at me. I could see them, their faces peering into my soul. They knew. They knew what I knew. I quickened my pace, but I couldn't get free of them. Every corner I turned, there was another twisted smile waiting for me. I ran the remainder of the hall to my door. Once safely inside my room, I double-checked to make sure the door was locked—or was it triple-checked? I closed the window and locked it as well. Jeremy was likely still fast asleep when I crept into bed. I sat and stared at the ceiling for what felt like years. The noises wouldn't leave me in peace, and the shadows taunted me. Darkness consumed every corner of the room until I finally allowed myself to be consumed by it as well.

I woke with a sweaty start. My alarm clock read 6:14 am. Two nights a week I experienced these phenomena, and I always woke up at exactly 6:14 on the nights that it occurred. It had haunted me for weeks. Why that time? What significance did that hold? Jeremy thought that I was crazy for thinking there could be any reason behind it, but I proved him wrong when I looked to the Bible. 2 Corinthians 6:14 says, "Be ye not unequally yoked together with unbelievers: for what fellowship hath righteousness with unrighteousness? and what communion hath light with darkness?" While I didn't know exactly what to make of it, I knew one thing: it had to mean something. It had to. The questions it posed for me were in themselves frightening, but fear is necessary to understand.

Jeremy still thought I had lost it, but maybe he was the one who had lost it. Whatever "it" was. He just couldn't hear the noises because he wasn't special like I am. He wasn't chosen, like me. The ghosts didn't want him to know what I learned; he couldn't see what I could, and what I can still see.

I set my alarm once more, for around eight, and drifted off to sleep. I dreamt of the spirits and their quests for me. I knew what I had to do. I knew that Jeremy was in the way and that he couldn't fathom the thought of me knowing what I knew. He wasn't worthy.

"So that's how it happened. That's why we get to be buddies now." I looked to the heavily tattooed man on the bed across from my own. "Even though it's been a few months, I still have the visions most nights. Sometimes, I even hear the voices while I'm awake. But don't worry; I'll get out of here soon." I shot a look at the officer passing by the barred door. He hadn't heard me. If he had, he'd probably brushed it off as something he heard every day. He couldn't possibly know the truth. The truth about the temporary, corporeal world that we're imprisoned in. The truth that, imprisoned by the law or not, we're all inmates confined to this plane of existence, and it's my job to set us free.

Besides, it was just me and my new roommate with no ghosts to bother us and no noises to distract me from my destiny. The only distraction, really, was my new friend and cellmate, and if there's one thing I've learned from all of this, it's that I really hate distractions.

A hallway located on the first floor of the Brick.

CLEAN AS CRIMSON
KAITLIN "KATT" VILLANUEVA

THE DAY HAD finally come: my first ever college visit.

I was dead set on Alfred University, but my mom pestered me to come and see the place anyway. Upon walking through the campus, I loved the cozy feeling it gave me, almost as if I were exploring a mystical town from long ago with its ancient charm and grace. My legs danced as I admired the main street that harbored the brick academic buildings and dormitories. The deep crimson brick and tangling ivy cornering the walls further fueled my fantasy state. I knew deep down I needed to be here. And so I was, nearly half a year later.

While on the tour, we had walked through the Brick Dormitory, and I instantly fell in love with its architecture. It's odd for someone my age to have such an interest in architecture, but I'm an art student; what else is there to expect? I didn't know much about the infamous lore of the building and honestly didn't pay much attention to it. Such whisperings did not deter me from requesting to live there. Throughout the first week of classes, I would hear tall tales and brief historical anecdotes, but they did not make me love the place any less.

Until it came time to shower.

After a long first few days, I was excited to finally get a break from the anxiety of adapting to a new life as a college student. I emerged from my room with my clunky shower caddy in hand and black towel across my body. The squeak from my cheap flip flops could be heard through the empty hallway as I pushed the bathroom door open., My ears were greeted by the sound of water running: both showers were taken. Not knowing what to do, I ended up waiting back in my room for a while.

When I returned, the showers were both empty, so I took the one that seemed the cleanest. I set my caddy down on the hard plastic bench next to the shower before I looked at the knobs. They were not what I had in my shower back at home, so I mindlessly started twisting and turning both of them, hoping I'd get my desired temperature. After a bit, I tested the water with my hand before I hopped in.

It was your run of the mill shower. Nothing too fancy or really updated, but not far from what is expected of dorm quality. Regardless of its external features, it was able to give me the comfort and tranquility I desired. I felt at ease as I let my shoulders relax under the warm rain, wishing this singular moment could last longer. All was going fine until I felt a sudden burst of cold water. My body recoiled as I quickly reached for what may have been the hot water knob. I frantically turned it to its highest setting before getting back to my duties. Other than the freak cold spell, all went as expected. No boogie men were behind the curtain. No killer clowns came up from the drain. Nothing happened other than someone coming in to use the sink.

I think that might have been it! I know flushing the toilet can make the hot water in the shower flash, so maybe when someone uses the sink it snatches the hot water? I couldn't be so sure at the time.

I went back to my room, setting my now wet caddy down on the floor before I started to dry myself off.

"How was your shower?" My roommate asked, her eyes glued to her computer screen.

"Kind of annoying, honestly. Trying to figure the knobs out got on my nerves but I ended up getting the hang of it, I guess. I did get paralyzed by a flash of cold water."

I moseyed around the room, putting my school things away.

"Huh...that's strange," she retorted.

Not much else was brought up about the matter. If she knew something, she would've definitely told me. Even though we had just met months before I moved in, I felt that I could trust her and confide in her if I needed to.

Once the first introductory week wrapped up, I felt relieved that I had the weekend to explore the campus and restore my frazzled brain. I decided to take another shower before starting off my day. I wasn't thinking much about the odd cold chill I got from the last one, so I went in pretty blind. Once I was ready, I turned the knobs, set my stuff down and hopped in. I started my routine again with little interruption. This time, however, the water changed temperature repeatedly. I spent more time messing with the controls than actually getting clean. No one else was in the bathroom with me, so I knew it wasn't someone pulling a prank on me.

Defeated, with only half washed hair and one leg shaved, I got out of the shower. I couldn't take the back and forth.

Hot then cold.

Hot then cold.

Hot then cold.

It was driving me nuts! I came back to the room to find my roommate still asleep, so I tried my hardest to stay quiet. Though fuming with anger, I composed myself; I didn't want to wake her with my truck-driver talk.

I sat, soaking wet, in the uncomfortable wooden desk chair as I tried to work out what I could do. I still wanted to get clean, but the shower wasn't cooperating whatsoever. I thought, "Maybe if I go back after a bit, it'll get back to normal. I could've messed up the controls, or maybe there was something wrong with the water heater." Determined, I went back to the bathroom and claimed the shower opposite to the one I was using before.

I turned the water on, both hot and cold, and waited for a few seconds. The base of the shower almost instantly filled with water.

"You have to be kidding me!"

I rushed to turn the water off but nothing was working. Regardless of which direction I turned the knobs, the water would not stop. It began to flood the floor not only in the shower but also the rest of the bathroom. Panicked, I ran out of the bathroom and knocked on the RA's door. I assume he was still sleeping when I knocked, because when he opened the door, he seemed very groggy. After I explained to him what happened, he promised to call the custodian on duty. I went back to my room and slipped my pajamas back on before sitting down on my bed.

What did I do wrong? The first shower hates me and the other one just doesn't work. Am I the problem? I've heard no one else complaining except me...

Another week went by before I tried it out again. I was unsure if I should just go to another floor; I didn't want to seem like I was intruding. I woefully went back to the dreaded "Hot, Cold" stall on my floor. As my feet squeaked down the hallway, I heard small whispers from every crevice of the walls saying,

"Don't go! What're you doing? Just leave!"

My head snapped back over my shoulder. The source of the whisperings was probably my imagination, though they sounded very convincing. I knew I was too much in my head. It's a shower. What's so hard about it?

I walked into the bathroom and to the stall, performing the same song and dance I've been trying to master for what seemed like years now.

I just want things to go right.

I waited a few seconds for the water to warm up before stepping in, hanging the towel on the designated hook, and setting my caddy down on the seat. I sighed as I once again fell back into the state of calmness I had been dreaming of. The warmth of the water brought me home. My nervousness seemed to wash down the drain as I stood, my eyes closed as I enjoyed each second of the shower. Upon opening my eyes, however, I saw a red puddle beneath my feet. The crimson liquid covered my entire body and hair; not an inch of my skin was bare of the horror. The only thing that could be heard aside from the showerhead was a petrified scream escaping my throat. I got my towel and ran straight out of the bathroom and to my room, dripping red all over the hallway and on the new white shag carpet that covered the beat up brown floor in my room. My voice shuddered as I tried my best to explain to my roommate what had happened, and all she responded with was laughter.

"What were you doing in there? I have no clue what the hell you're talking about!"

Her disbelief made me burst into tears as I ran out of the room to go back to the bathroom and clean myself off in the sink. But there was not a spot of red on me or even on the floor. The shower had stopped, and nothing was in the drain other than the water from someone who had been in there prior to me.

THE NIGHT ROUND
KAZIMERAS TAGGART

FINALLY! THE END of the spring semester, the end of having daily rounds, the end of getting woken up by people's issues, and the end of this "haunted" building. Not that it bothers me much. My only job this week? Make sure people are moved out and left with no belongings behind. It's a bit of a pain, having to check each room, but I manage because it is my job, and I do get paid well enough to continue being an RA.

I already searched the first-floor rooms yesterday and no unusual events occurred on that floor. Again, have any notable events ever appeared other than finding underage kids smoking marijuana or drinking alcohol? The Common room is said to be haunted, but I've never personally believed the stories about the Brick. The creepiest thing that ever happened to me was someone walking on the first-floor roof. You know, the fire escape roof? Besides purposely scaring others, there's nothing paranormal. Y'know, I think people like that should get a life.

There are three RA's: Lukas, Elias, and me. Lukas is pretty shy; he doesn't like Elias either. Lukas says he's been in Alfred for forever, and I guess that means born and raised here, although he's mentioned the long journey to here from across the sea, so maybe he's an immigrant. He's also mentioned he's interested in medicine, even though Alfred University is twenty percent an art school; do we even have a medical program here? Anyway, he rarely speaks about himself, but when he

47

does he always talks as if he won't get to accomplish his dreams of helping people or saving their lives. I'm sure he will one day! He's just gotta have hope!

Lukas and I are close, while Elias rarely does his job, acts like a prick, and is usually joining the other students in smoking pot. Lukas and I can't fathom how he even became an RA, and sometimes we play pranks on him too, since he never even saw us do them. Lukas is a genius! He's impressive at scaring others without notice. It's hard to sneak around because the floor creaks at every step, so whenever we manage a good one on Elias, it's super rewarding.

Although Lukas and Elias always avoid each other, it seems like they could eventually get along. If Lukas would ever actually talk to Elias.

Along with the creaky floors, the running water is only consistently warm on the first floor, while the third floor doesn't get any warm water. We must have horrible water pressure. Even the second floor is fussy, but the first floor is a luxury! But don't tell anyone, alright? It will be... our secret. Yes, our secret! Especially since I live on the first floor. This isn't important, but it's a fun fact!

I start my morning round, checking the supposedly empty rooms and seeing if anyone is to be in trouble or fined for failing to complete the rules given to them. I'm turning the corner when—

"Ow!" I smack into Lukas. He's built like a brick, reliable as concrete.

"Oh, sorry, Toni, I turned the corner too fast," Lukas says, flustered and red-faced.

"Goodness, no! It's fine, Lukas! I was in a rush to get my rounds done so I could relax before trying to finish my final essay."

He thinks for a second and asks me, "For what class?"

"Um, I think the literature class on William Shakespeare? I'm too stressed to remember."

"That sounds rough, unless you're into Shakespeare or are Shakespeare."

"Hehehe, yeah..." Suddenly, it's an awkward silence that I can't figure out how to fix. Awkward, that is until Elias appears, and Lukas just kind of vanishes upon hearing Elias's booming voice.

As he approaches, Elias sarcastically says, "Ah, well... well, if it isn't our favorite RA of the entire Brick residence, Toni."

"If it isn't your royal hind-ass," I retort with a sly grin. We both laugh, and I ask Elias when he plans on making his rounds tonight.

"I did them yesterday," he says, "and I know it's a daily thing, but can't you take over for tonight?... I promised to get the good stuff for the party. You know how hard it is to find good helium balloons?"

I just facepalm and agree to take over his rounds for the day; always covering for him is gonna come back to get me.

So, I reluctantly do midday rounds and check the floors from the ground up; that way, I can double-check on the way down. The building is shaped like an uppercase "T," which makes it easy to navigate.

I stop at a room where both residents have moved out, so I take one of their keys and enter to see if they followed the protocols.

They forgot to unplug their printer, didn't lock the window, and left me three bags of trash. Ugh! Can't people follow the rules at least once? I begrudgingly grab the stupid bag and walk to the dumpster. I literally just throw them at the container and turn around. As I do, I see someone staring at me from the window on the third floor. Creepy much? I just wave and avoid eye contact.

I have to take the trash out for a few more rooms which means each of the kids gets fined about fifty bucks. I could be nice and let them off, but... I really don't feel like being nice today, maybe because this is the sixth room I've found trash in, and I'm still on the first floor. They just leave their bags of garbage and some gross unmentionables sitting there. I can feel Elias snickering at me now. He probably knew this would happen, and that's why he asked. I couldn't have predicted this, though, because I'm usually oblivious to certain things. I should've known better with him...

Now that I've finished the second floor with only two trips to the great dumpster of trash, all that's left is the third floor. I trot up the stairs to the third floor and am starting my usual routine when I hear footsteps above me. Is someone in the attic? I go over to the door leading upstairs and turn the knob. The door opens, but it should be locked; now the custodian is in trouble. Why is everyone so problematic for me? At least Lukas isn't problematic. If he was, I'd go insane! He's just sweet as butterscotch.

The floors groan and creak beneath my feet as I ascend to the attic; the lights are on, but when walking around, I find no one. Could it be a rat? After all, it's an old building. I turn to leave and see Lukas; I scream, and he jumps back.

"Whoa, whoa, whoa!" he says, putting his hands up. "Calm down, it's just me. I saw you going up, and I got worried someone else could be up here. I heard footsteps."

God, I must be an idiot! I mentally slap myself.

"Goodness me, I'm sorry, I didn't mean to scream... I just didn't expect anyone to actually come up here too, y'know, since it's forbidden?"

"I understand. It's just, how did you get up here without a key?"

"It—it was unlocked?"

"The custodian locked it about an hour ago, Toni, so how could it be unlocked?

Unless you have a key or someone else broke into the attic."

"He could've come back for something and forgot to lock it back up?"

"Or maybe something supernatural unlocked it. I mean, it makes sense, considering all the history, all the deaths from the influenza pandemic in 1918, and the fact that the entire third floor burned down and was rebuilt. There's also all the students who claim to have heard weird things."

"Why would I believe in something I've never seen?" I roll my eyes. "Anyway, I need to finish lunchtime rounds; I'll have to do this again later because Elias is having a party." I shake my hands with sarcastic jazziness, and it gets a laugh from Lukas.

"Alright, just be careful of the ghosts you oh-so-don't-believe-in. You'll upset them!" Then he sticks his tongue out.

And with that, he winks and leaves me to finish my routine checks. Before I can follow him, he's already gone, so I check the other rooms. I spot the person who was watching me from the window earlier, but then my phone buzzes; I see it's just a game notification. When I look back up only seconds later, the person has left with no sound of doors closing or footsteps. People are way too skinny nowadays, not making any noise walking on these old floors.

I do get a weird feeling, but I ignore it, and since I've finished, I make my way down the stairs, and then I lie down and end up taking a nap.

A few hours later, I wake up and look at the clock: it's already 11pm! How did I sleep this long? Oh, sugar honey iced tea! I've missed the usual times to make my rounds, so I guess I'll do them now when everyone else is either asleep, finishing their final essays, or partying. Essays... I forgot to type my essay... now I only have one day to finish writing it... now I'm stressed again. I've been running on five hours of sleep for a week now. The number of all-nighters is killing me slowly.

Whatever, I have to recheck the rooms and see if anyone's left since lunchtime.

First floor? Nothing!

Second floor? Two rooms, one trash bag filled with an ungodly volume of tissues, and a kid crying in the hall over their failed finals. I console them only briefly before continuing onto the third floor because the faster I get this done, the faster I can get back to my gosh darn work!

The lights are dim on the third floor, and this late at night, it's relatively dark up here. I go over to the first room, and suddenly a door slams open. I jump a bit at the noise, but I go to investigate and find that the slammed door leads to an unoccupied room. No one has ever lived in this room while I've been a resident here. It's my job to check it out, so I enter the room; it's just a very dusty room, nothing even creepy, I mean, it's just...

SLAM!

"Who just slammed the door on me?" I yell. "You're going to be in a lot of trouble!"

I try the door and the lock, but they won't budge! I yell again, but no one comes. I try a few more times again at the door but ultimately fail.

I reluctantly sit down on the dusty bed and take out my phone, hoping I'm in an area of the building where the Wi-Fi works. I have bars, but not enough Wi-Fi. I try texting Elias to help me out, but he replies with a laughing emoji and an LOL.

"Great," I sigh.

Squeak, squeak.

Is there a mouse in here with me? Then, more squeaking, and I look down to see many beady eyes looking up at me. I scream and stand on the bed. I need to get out now!

"Please, anyone, let me out! *Please!*"

The mice crawl up to me, and just when I think that their grimy diseased bodies are going to touch me, they vanish. What the hell just happened?

The door swings open, so I run out and slam it behind me. I don't even have time to catch my breath before I see the same person I found staring at me earlier is at the other end of the hall. They start laughing, and I stare back at them. The person only smiles, smiles, and smiles at me. Recalling that I've just run away from a mouse infestation, I suddenly laugh too, for how could that have actually happened? The person laughs harder, an unnatural laugh that stops me in my tracks. When I look at them again, they aren't at the end of the hall but a mere ten feet away.

"S-s-stay—stay back! I don't know who you are, but you can end the little act now, alright?"

No response; just the laughter getting louder and louder. How is no one else hearing this? I regain my composure and slowly walk backward away from this person, this... thing.

As I creep back, I hear something behind me. What do I do? Turn around and look or keep facing this laughing thing?

I have to gather my courage. Instead of looking away completely, I turn to look behind me, and when there's nothing there, I quickly turn back to the other end of the hall. But the person is gone.

I didn't nap as well as I'd like to believe, it seems. It's just gotta be my tired brain and Lukas's teasing about the building being haunted. Yes... yes, that's it... That's gotta be it...

I run down the stairs to the second floor, but as I quickly glance at the room numbers, they all start with three; I turn back to the stairs I just came down, but they have vanished. Looking forward, I see the stairs are down the hall.

Did I just imagine going down the stairs instead? No...

I run down the stairs again, and again, ending up down the hall away from them every time. I'm trapped in a loop or something. Could this be a dream? A lucid dream, yes, yes, I'm very much asleep, and this is all an unpleasant dream! I'm perfectly sane; I'm mentally stable. I'm not crazy or stressed or panicked. *I'm fine.*

I need to break out of this dream then! I could try jumping out the window! It seems safe, even if I could die. It seems like the sanest idea I've ever thought of.

Perfect! A perfect plan! I run to the nearest window and throw it open. I crawl to the edge and jump.

I return to the same spot yet again, so I start trying everything, going through doors, the window again, and back up to the attic, but I cannot escape this hellish nightmare. I finally sit down in the corner, keeping my head on my knees. The person is there again, and they aren't laughing. Just smiling again.

"What? What do you want from me?" I sob. "I'm just an English major! I cannot give you anything... other than help with grammar! Please let me go..."

The figure starts walking over to me, but they seem kind this time, for their face has softened. Still smiling, the person reaches their hand out to me.

I grab it, relief washing over me. "Are you letting me leave?"

Still no response; just a giant grin. Holding my hand, they walk me over to the window and point to the concrete below.

"You want me to jump? I've already tried that; it didn't work! You'll see! I'll show you, and then you'll actually help me leave, Right? Oh great, thank you."

I can finally leave. Once I show them that this doesn't work, I'll be free, and then I'll be able to go back downstairs. So I crawl onto the ledge and stand up in the window frame, looking down at the ground I've tried to jump to multiple times today. One more time won't hurt. No, not at all. I'm stepping to the ledge when someone tries to grab me, and I lose balance. I feel my body fall, but then suddenly come to a stop.

"Toni, what are you doing? Are you crazy?" Lukas's scream returns me to reality. "How did you manage to get this window open?" He pulls me up and back inside. "Are you okay? Are you hurt? Are you—"

"They seemed very reasonable. Was she joking with me?"

"They? Who's they? There are no residents left on the third floor. They vacated last night. Other than that, you're safe now, so calm down. Please, just breathe."

I sit there and do what he says.

"Was I sleepwalking?"

"Sleepwalking? You were doing rounds, weren't you? I doubt sleepwalking is the answer for almost jumping out a window that's broken and doesn't open… until today that is… but are you alright? That's the most important question to me right now."

So, it wasn't a dream? I giggle, and he looks concerned. I stand up and just cackle at him. It's the same horrible laugh as the figure had before that hell started.

"Alright? Am I *alright*? Of course, I'm alright! You are one funny guy, Lukas, I'll give you that! I'll see you tomorrow."

"Yeah, tomorrow…" he says, standing there and looking a bit sad as I walk downstairs, now that I've finally escaped.

As I make it onto the first floor, I see Elias in the common room, smoking a bong by himself with the substances stolen from the other students.

"You know you can't smoke inside the building, right?" I'm half annoyed and half glad to see him.

He blows the smoke into my face.

"Eh, whatever. You would've loved the party, by the way; I held a helium competition to see whose voice went the highest."

"You didn't see me sleepwalking? Lukas says I wasn't but… it seems logical… unless I'm just that sleep-deprived."

"Sleepwalking? Lukas? Who's Lukas? Are you sure I'm the one that's high right now?"

"Are you that stupid that you don't know the name of the other RA, Peter Lukas? My best friend who I'm always with?"

"… I guess you really were sleepwalking, sweets. We're the only two RA's in the Brick."

Seeing me confused, he realizes I wasn't making a joke.

"I'm serious, Elias," I insist. "He saved me from jumping out the window."

"Jumping out the window? That's not important. What's important is that I'm telling you… Toni, my sweet, there hasn't been a third RA in the Brick this semester, I swear on my bong. I'll even show you how crazy you sound." He sighs. "I really didn't wanna show you the records I stole from the attic earlier for my history assignment, but here, read away!"

And he shows me the list of every resident to ever live in the Brick. Not a single Peter Lukas has been here since the influenza pandemic. The log says he died from the flu, 1918.

It's 2021.

Red Coat

Sydney Barnett

THE FIRST TIME he had seen her, he supposed, was when things were really getting lonely.

Winter was finally beginning to overstay its welcome, and the air froze to the bone, never caring much for positive numbers when the nights came. Campus was often covered in a new blanket of snow each day, if not a blanket of ice or slush. Everybody, from students to professors, was expected to pick up from where they had last left off as the stress of classes returned once more. The sun was rarely around, and moments of freedom were sparse. It was simply Valerie and his classes.

Valerie wouldn't consider himself a special guy. He was just another art major residing in the Brick, trying to swim through the tides of Foundations classes as he considered next year's medium options. Surely, with such a common story, he would have made connections. He would have found a group of friends, or at least a pack of study buddies who would help him through the workload. But that wasn't the case, and, frankly, it was almost how Valerie liked it. He was used to it, after all. Being around people was nerve-wracking and chaotic. One could never tell when things would fall apart, when drama would rear its ugly head or when Valerie would make a fool of himself and shatter a perfectly good relationship.

So he kept to himself.

Even when he shared a room with James Everett, who left when the spring semester came.

Even when he heard the noise from the common room, the hearty laughter and upbeat small talk from the friend groups who had woven themselves together.

Even when he was neck-deep in assignments, just barely being able to drag himself to shore again before the fall semester concluded.

Even when *she* had shown up for the first time.

It had been another night of work that Valerie absolutely despised. For the third time that week, all he could bring himself to do during his studio time was stare for what felt like hours. His mind had yet again drawn a blank on how to approach that damned sculpture project, and his hands refused to work without a proper plan. It was only when the hunger headache began to kick in that Valerie finally dragged himself out of Harder Hall. With his brain numb and his heavy art kit digging into his shoulder, he made his way towards Main Street. The dining halls were closed, and he had no real meals back at his dorm, so getting food from town was really his only option.

That night should have been normal. Valerie's walk in the cold should have been uneventful. He should have stopped at the Chinese restaurant, walked back to the Brick and crashed for the night, awaiting another day of wasted work time.

He shouldn't have been so nosy walking up Saxon Drive. Maybe he wouldn't have ever even noticed her.

Valerie's eyes wandered anyways. It was either that, or have the cold night wind digging into his eyes. He was walking up the sidewalk, passing by Stonehenge, when he spotted red. Vibrant red. It caused him to freeze for a second and stare down through the clearing of trees, down across to the other side of the stream below him. Looking closer, he could see someone standing in front of the tunnel there, their unusually bright coat seeming to glow in the dark.

Valerie blinked. The other person was no longer there.

"What…?" Valerie murmured to himself. He shook his head and began walking back to the Brick again. Reaching the main door, he fumbled for his keys in his pocket, noticing that his hands seemed awfully numb for how long he had been outside. He unlocked the door, stumbled up the stairs, and made his way down the hall to his room. God, *everything* felt numb. It was only when he finally stepped into his room again that he realized just how *cold* he was.

Valerie kicked off his boots and collapsed onto his bed, content to lay there for the rest of time. It was cozy and warm, nothing like the outside. He rolled onto his side, and pulled his phone out of his coat pocket. He checked the time.

12:39 a.m.

…Wait.

12:39? But I left around…

Valerie shook his head. He was probably just misremembering again. That happened a lot nowadays. Everything seemed to move so fast lately; the days just bled together, leaving little room for him to think much anymore. He supposed, though, that getting a bite to eat would help, even if just for the moment. With a tired sigh, Valerie forced himself up off the soft bed sheets and towards the desk he had placed his bag of Chinese food on. Grabbing the bag, he noticed that it was extremely cold. Only a sliver of warmth radiated from the box of sweet and sour chicken inside.

"Could be worse, I guess," Valerie mumbled, taking the box out of the bag. "At least I'm eating *something* worthwhile…"

He grabbed his plastic fork and began eating for the first time in hours, pushing the red coat out of his mind.

**

It was 3:30 in the morning. Again.

Valerie was just lucky to have actually gotten everything done this time. With one final click of his computer mouse, he turned in his last assignment and leaned back onto the pillows behind him. Sleep was tempting, but he knew he couldn't give in yet. His laptop was still open, and, as gross as it sounded, he hadn't brushed his teeth or washed his face yet. After laying on his bed for far too long, he finally got up and grabbed his laptop, closing it shut and putting it back on the desk where it belonged. Picking up his shower caddy and washcloth, he left for the bathroom.

The halls were empty like they always were. Valerie could still vaguely hear a few other people from inside their rooms, playing music or talking amongst each other, but they were out of sight. He didn't know any of them, anyways. Taking in the dimly-lit space, he simply walked to the bathroom and got ready for bed. The quiet was nice, but he knew it wouldn't last forever. He would have to go to bed and wake up to more noise eventually. On his way back to his dorm, he stopped.

Valerie's room was on the end of the one hall near a window where he could look out onto the road in front of the Brick. He always enjoyed staring out of that window at night. Looking out it then, he could see snow gently falling to the ground below, which was already covered in a thin layer of the stuff. As much as he wanted the snow to go away, he couldn't help but feel calmed by its presence. The soft glow of the streetlamps dotted along that part of campus gave off a dream-like vibe, and the way they lit up the ground made everything feel peaceful. Everything was calm. Nobody would be around that night except for the lights and snow. Nobody would be there to ruin the scene. Nobody would be there at all.

Valerie blinked. His heart dropped.

The red coat was back.

The person was now standing on the sidewalk in front of Herrick Library, right across the street. They were staring at him now, there was no doubt about it. Valerie couldn't make out their face, but he knew. He couldn't make out anything about them at all, actually. That damn red coat was the only thing that stuck out amid the darkness gathered outside Herrick. Why did it stick out so much? Why were they staring? Why—

"Are you okay?"

Valerie jumped and spun around. A girl was standing there, staring at him with concern written all over her face.

"I—uh…" Valerie began to sputter, nervously glancing back out the window again. The red coat was gone. Taking a quick breath to calm himself, he managed to finally answer, "Ye-yeah. I'm fine. Why're you asking?"

"You've kinda just been…standing there, dude," the girl said.

"Am I not allowed to look at the snow?"

"Yeah, but for like… a *half hour?*"

Valerie froze.

"…A *what?*" he gasped.

"Well, maybe? All I'm saying is that you were standing there for…" the girl began to speak again. But Valerie couldn't hear her anymore. A half hour? He wasn't there for that long, surely. It had to have been a couple minutes at most. He grasped his phone, sitting in the pocket of his pajama pants.

Only a few minutes, only a few minutes, Valerie thought. This girl had to have been mistaken, somehow. Besides, how would have she known how long he was out here for? She was lying for—

4:03 a.m.

Oh.

"...Are you o——?"

"*Well, goodnight, then!*" Valerie blurted out, practically flinging himself into his dorm room. His hands raced as he locked the door, hit the lights, and slammed his closet door shut. His heart fluttered as its pace seemed to quicken with every passing second. All he could do was drag himself back to his bed and curl up on top of the blankets.

He had been standing there—for a half hour. Same place, same position. *A half hour.*

What the hell is wrong with me?

***

They were surely beginning to whisper behind his back now.

If the days had been blurring together before, then there was nothing but one long, continuous stretch of time now. The words "day" and "night" meant nothing anymore. The clocks would sometimes betray Valerie faster than his mind could, though trusting either of them was a dumb move at best and a risky one at worst.

It was all because of that damn red coat.

Every time, without fail, Valerie would see it just as time got hazy. He knew better than to trust windows anymore, since it would always be watching him from somewhere, staring him down through darkness and snow flurries. He could only guess how many times he met the thing's theoretical eyes and stared like a lunatic into the distance, never moving, never waking, until someone or something interrupted the exchange. While ol' "Red Coat" was typically the one to end things, it was still common for Valerie to wake to the sensation of being poked or shook by another student. He wasn't sure which ending left him feeling worse.

The other students had distanced themselves from him even more now. He knew they had. He could see the concerned pity in their eyes as he walked by. He could see the way they shuffled away from him as he took his place during demos. He could see it all. He could see it all clearly. They all thought he was crazy, and there wasn't a damn thing he could do to prove otherwise.

Even now, in the studio, Valerie could feel the eyes of Eric Grayson and Violet Cassilio boring into the back of his head. They were the only other people here at one in the morning, after all, trying to wrap things up before the deadline in seven hours.

"—*Bitch!*" Valerie yelped as hot glue stuck to his fingers. Again. He couldn't help but toss the glue gun a foot or two away from him as he shook his hand, desperately trying to alleviate some of the pain. Luckily, the glue didn't take long to cool once it hit his skin. Wincing, he began to peel off the dry glue, hoping that he didn't take off too much skin in the process.

A small cough caught Valerie's attention. Whipping his head around, he could see Eric and Violet sitting at the other end of the space. If he was any dumber, Valerie would have totally missed Eric's brief stare. It was only for a second, but it was there. It was there.

"*What?*" Valerie snapped.

"Hm?" Violet hummed, turning towards him.

"Not you, *him.*"

"He's got his headphones in. Did you need him for—"

"No. It's *fine.*"

Violet gave Valerie that look again. The same look everyone had been giving him for the past week now.

"Are you—"

"*I'm fine! I'm fine! I'm absolutely fine!*" Valerie screamed, leaping to his feet. "All of this is fucking bullshit! Stop looking at me like that!"

"I'm... sorry?" Violet slowly responded. Eric, the moron he was, finally seemed to notice him again. They were both staring now. They were both staring at an adult throwing a temper tantrum.

Valerie huffed and stormed off towards the bathrooms. He couldn't do this anymore. He just couldn't. All he wanted was for things to be over. This assignment, the isolation, the *Red Coat*. This was it. He was going insane and failing out of college. No one would ever believe him about the Red Coat. He was the only one who saw it, after all. He'd be shipped back home to his parents or sent to a mental institution. At this point, he couldn't quite say which one would be worse.

As his vision gradually got blurrier, Valerie kept his eyes glued to the ground. He couldn't risk another staring episode again. He'd never get this assignment done if he did. He made sure to focus on his footsteps, one foot in front of the other, as his shoes thumped against the ground. He was almost to the end of the windows lining the studio space.

Valerie froze. He knew why, but he kept his eyes to the ground.

Why are you here? he mentally asked the Red Coat staring at him.

He forced himself to take a step.

Why are you doing this to me?

Another step.

What did I ever do to you?

Another.

Who are you? What are you?

Another, another…

Get away from me, get away from me, get away from me, get away from me—

Another, another, another, another…

The cold wind hit Valerie's face before he knew where he was. He was outside of Harder, but he wasn't there long; he dashed along the icy sidewalks, never bothering to look up. The chill went straight to his bones. The only choice he had was to keep moving. He had to go.

The ground became unfamiliar, however. This wasn't the sidewalk to the Brick, Valerie knew that much. He had no idea where he was going, but the crackle of ice gave him a good indication. He froze for a second. His heart was pounding in his chest as lightheadedness fogged up his brain. He couldn't move anymore, no matter how hard he tried.

Valerie went against his better judgment and looked up. He was staring into the tunnels by Stonehenge. Even now, in the darkness, he could see it. The Red Coat stood a few yards away, silently judging him like it always did.

"… What… do you… *want?*" Valerie rasped, trying to ignore the way his voice cracked. His body felt stiff, but at least he was aware of it now. Although, he was *also* aware of something else.

The Red Coat was getting closer. But it never seemed to actually move. With every passing second, Valerie could see it a little clearer. He began to see the stains and tears along the vibrant fabric. Even closer, he could make out a hint of skin along the Red Coat's shadowy silhouette. Everything around the two of them seemed to be getting darker.

It was only then that Valerie realized that the Red Coat wasn't the one moving. He was.

He couldn't feel his legs anymore. He couldn't feel any part of his body anymore. All he could do was stare like he always did, watching the Red Coat gradually come closer. The coat's tears became increasingly prominent, and he could see that some of its buttons were missing. It seemed to be a rather old coat, not just in condition, but in style as well. This became more apparent as the dirtied furs around the neck of the coat emerged from the darkness, outlining just how tall the neck actually was.

The figure finally leaned in towards him, and, as Valerie's stomach dropped, her decaying face pressed up against his. Infected lacerations covered her grey visage, her eyes so cloudy he could barely see the remains of her broken pupils. Her torn mouth seemed to smile as she moved her crooked jaw and haphazardly swung her ice-cold limbs around him. He would have vomited at her rotting stench, but the world didn't feel real anymore.

Valerie's hand was able to move again. It moved alongside hers. He shouldn't have known such things. But he knew many things now. So many things.

Valerie knew that this woman was dead. He knew that he could only move when she wanted him to. He knew that this body wouldn't be his anymore. They knew he would be dead soon. *She* knew that she would have a chance to return again. She knew that her opportunity was right here, right in her long-forgotten arms.

She would be able to finish what she started.

All she had to do…

…

All she had to do…

…

…

There was a scream—a raw, frightened scream.

The snow came into view again. The ground was cold. Another person was standing there. Their muffled words seeped into the ringing air, but nothing they said could really be made out. It was unclear who they were even talking to. They seemed to be alone.

Another person popped up, mere inches away. "...alive!" they said. "Jas...e's alive...!" The other person bounded over and said something back. As the view became less and less blurry, the concern on their faces became more and more apparent. Something had happened. But with the way their voices were still muddying together, one could only guess what that was.

The good thing, though, was that it was starting to get a little warmer now, even if it was because the one guy had gotten a bit *too* close for comfort now. But it was whatever. Any heat would do at this point.

"Help's on the way," the guy said, clear as day. "Hang in there, man. It's okay, you're okay."

God, he was getting annoying now. He talked too much. Luckily, if this so-called "help" got here soon enough, he wouldn't be around much longer. Besides, things seemed to be getting better. Nothing appeared blurry anymore. Noise wasn't muffled or distorted. The warmth... *oh the warmth...*

She hadn't felt warmth in a long time...

Two Thirteen
S. K. Sage

WHEN WE STARTED living in the Brick, my roommate worried that she wouldn't be able to relax. She told me that she didn't want to mess with ghosts, or demons, or whatever else made the rounds in Alfred University folklore. Luckily for her, despite the many hours she spent within the hall, she never saw anything like that.

But whether or not I did, I'll leave that judgement up to you.

This story is just a part of a larger tale, but until I am ready, it will end where it ends.

**

We tried to keep our window open whenever we could, even during the spring semester; the heater in our room was so stifling, we would have suffocated otherwise. The window never stayed open long, though.

The way our room was oriented, any type of breeze would cause the old door to shudder violently. I'll be honest; it took a while for the two of us to realize that it was the wind and not an RA. The hammering was almost human, but once we closed the window, it almost always stopped. Almost.

We took shifts in checking the door. She would always check in the morning, and I would check at night, after we shared a confused look about who the hell could be pounding on our door during the designated 'Quiet Hours.'

We would always open the door to an empty hall.

***

Her bed was beside the door, mine beside the window. She had the better night's sleep, as it took me a long time to get used to the fact that the nights here were never dark and never quiet.

With the amber hues from streetlamps and headlights, the reflections from the colored LEDs and televisions in my neighbors' windows, it wasn't rare to go to sleep to muffled conversation and passing shadows.

This was why, some nights, I found it strange that the silhouette of a person was plastered on the wall of our room and found it even stranger that it never moved for as long as my tired eyes stared at it.

Paranoid, I would shift in my creaking bed to look but find nothing casting the shadow. Nothing, even still, when I would turn back to where it had been.

***

For a time, it was just shadows and knocking. Then, it was in that space between dreaming and consciousness that I heard him; his voice so clear that I don't think I'll ever forget the sound.

It was as if he knelt by my bed and whispered into my ear, "Hello, Alicia."

He didn't always talk to me. When he did, it was never when I was fully awake; it was always in that half-asleep state when your head gets light.

***

But there was one night, and it haunts me to this day, when I woke up at some godforsaken hour. I hadn't bothered to check my phone, though I could tell from the window that it was probably 2 or 3 in the morning.

The room was quiet with the white noise of our box fan and the once-in-a-while shuffling as my roommate slept. This quiet felt different, though, not like other nights.

My bed creaked, as it always did, when I sat up. My feet barely caressed the wooden floor as I let the sleep melt off me before I moved any further. I leaned forward—to stretch or put my head in my hands, I can't remember now—and saw something in the corner of my eye.

The door was open.

I turned my head fully, and I saw a tall, tall man with his head bent low and a wide, sharp grin upon his face, one hand slack against his body, the other on the doorknob.

I couldn't bring myself to do anything except stare at his shadowed figure against the dim hallway lights. His smile never faded, never, for as long as we stared at each other.

When he closed the door and I heard the click of the latch, only then was able to move, like a hypnotist's snap. Wracked with nausea, I checked the lock on our side to find it was in place.

I unlocked it, the adrenaline making it sound so much louder than it was. But throwing the door open and standing on the threshold brought no consolation. Whoever he was, he was gone.

That morning, I was exhausted from staying up to ensure he didn't come back. When my roommate woke, I asked her if she'd ever heard the door rattle or open at night, if she'd heard walking, or what.

"No," she said. "Once I'm asleep, I'm asleep. Why?"

"Just want to make sure I'm not waking you up," I lied.

There was something unsaid between us, but I knew she never saw the Tall Man. She probably thought I was just feeling overly anxious, that I was on the edge of burnout. In fact, I know that's what she thought, because she was always making sure I was getting enough sleep and taking breaks after that conversation.

That night, I heard his voice again.

From the bedside, he murmured, "Thank you for keeping our secret, Alicia."

BECAUSE HE COULD NOT SEE
Monica Nowik

ANYONE WHO HAS glasses will tell you that you cannot comfortably wear a mask and still reasonably see for jackshit, especially when it's cold AF outside. Well, that's fine and all to be blinded for a few seconds, but what if you missed something really important during those few seconds?

You're probably thinking, "Tyler, you sound kind of salty about this", and you know what? Yeah, I am. You want to know why?

See, I was trying to join the Paranormal club on campus, hoping to get in on some of that ghost action, but first I had to pass the test of getting a ghost on camera. My roommate Dylan said that the president was just messing with me. They don't know what they're talking about though; Dylan doesn't really get my interest in ghosts no matter how many times I try to explain it to them, but whatever.

That's how I came to be in front of the Brick on that fine blustery Saturday evening, my phone held at ready. Dylan had come with me, probably worried for my sanity, and when Skylar saw us lurking outside the Brick, he'd joined too, and now we also had Julia with us for some reason.

The reason I had to wait outside the Brick was because I'd landed the worst lot in life and been assigned to Kruson my freshman year, which sucked major ass. I mean, the Brick was *known* for being infested with ghost activity, and I somehow ended up in the building *next* to it? And the worst thing really was, the pandemic kept us from being allowed to go in any other dorms.

So the next best thing was to wait outside and see if a ghost popped up.

Dylan looked up at the sky. "It's starting to snow," they said. "Tyler, maybe we should try again tomorrow."

I rolled my eyes. "Alright, go inside if you're scared. If I leave now, I just know that a ghost will appear the second I turn around. Just... just give it a few more minutes."

"That's what you said an hour ago," Skylar muttered, and Julia snorted involuntarily.

I turned around and glared at the two of them, which wasn't super effective because the lower half of my face was covered in the Alfred colors of purple and gold, and my thick-framed glasses kept my eyebrows from being too expressive.

"Okay, okay," Julia said, raising her hands defensively. "We want to see a ghost too, you know."

I made a huffing noise and turned back to keeping a vigilant watch on the door. Even if I just got a glimpse of something inside... and could catch it on camera... that would be enough for me. Then I could really call myself a ghost-watcher instead of a Buzzfeed- Unsolved- Supernatural-watcher.

Something just inside the door of the Brick stirred. I tensed, my phone clutched tightly in my hand, finger poised over the record button. The door creaked...

I jumped violently as a girl flung the door open and stalked down the sidewalk past us, throwing us a suspicious look over her shoulder. I didn't blame her; we looked like a group of nerds ready to jump the first person out of the door and ask them if they'd heard about Dungeons and Dragons.

"Breathe, my guy," Dylan said, patting me empathetically on the shoulder. "Ya gotta relax."

"I *am* relaxed," I growled, trying to hide my annoyance but failing dismally.

Fuck, it was starting to get really cold out here. I wished I could put my gloves on, but then I couldn't have activated my phone's touchscreen.

"What's that?"

I glanced at Skylar. He was looking up at a second floor window, transfixed.

"I don't see anything," Julia said, irritation creeping around the edges of her voice. "I think I'm gonna go back to Bartlett. I have a paper due at midnight."

None of us were listening to Julia, because now Dylan and I had seen what Skylar had: something quickly moved away from the window, as if trying to hide from sight. I tapped my phone's screen before it went dark and started recording; I didn't want to miss the tiniest detail.

"I *still* don't *see* anything," Julia began again, but Dylan shushed her.

I was still staring at the window when I noticed a shadow move across the first-floor doorway; it was coming outside, and this time, I felt sure it wasn't a student. I couldn't see what was casting the shadow—it moved irregularly, almost pulsating, flickering in and out of existence.

I moved closer to the door, hunched and ready to pounce on—well, I didn't know quite what. My rapid breath started to fog up my glasses, but I ignored it.

"*Oh my god!*"

Dylan's scream was swallowed by a gust of wind that swept Julia's AU hat right off her head, and simultaneously, the door swung open; whether the wind came from within the Brick or from outside, I'd never know.

Stumbling backwards, I couldn't see a thing. My glasses were completely and utterly opaque with fog.

"*What the hell is that?*"

"I'm going, I'm not fucking doing this—"

The sound of running feet. Someone grabbing my arm to steady me. The Brick's front door slamming once again. Skylar whimpering. All these were lost to me as I slowly reached up and pulled my glasses off, Dylan's blurry face coming into view.

Dylan stared at the now innocently closed door, terror etched onto their face. "What...what *was* that?"

"I don't even want to know." Skylar's shoulders trembled.

"What did you guys see?" I asked blankly.

"I couldn't even describe it."

"It didn't look human."

"Massive amounts of bad vibes."

"Like a corpse."

Slowly, I looked down at my phone, still clutched in one numb hand. There, on the screen, I could see that all I'd managed to capture was a blurry photo of Julia's feet.

Whatever my friends saw that night, it must have been traumatizing, as none of them had similar versions of what the shadow's true form had really looked like. It isn't fucking fair, because *I'm* the one who needed the evidence.

Skylar says that next time, I should tape my glasses to my mask so they won't fog up. I'll look stupid, but it's a small price to pay. I'll have to be sure to thank him if it works.

Harder Hall, one of the homes of the School of Art and Design.

Paper Thin
Wyatt A. Zindle

THE MAN HAD spent the unhealthy majority of his waking hours working in the studio. Though he typically loved work that demanded such intense focus, his brain was fried, and his short-tempered joints were complaining.

On his way through the snow back to his dorm, the man thought to himself, in the tone of a bitter, wife-hating old man, how he planned to throw a fit should he arrive at the studio the next day and find his work toppled as he anticipated. If the first assignment of the first semester were to be ruined, he wouldn't know what to tell the professor.

He reminded himself that, if needed, he had photos of the work that he could substitute in at the critique. He'd have to remember to send the shots of the completed work to his family, but not tonight. That would only concern his mother with his habit of working all night.

Distracted in thought, he encountered in the snow a patch of comparatively shallow, slippery terrain that aimed to test his balance and his nerves, a test which he failed spectacularly.

The man stood back up and shot a scolding look at the sidewalk that had bested him. With the concoction of exhaust, stress, and a wearing-off energy drink in his system, he supposed it would have been a surprise if he had found a way to make it back in such darkness without slipping once. He continued and looked to the usual tranquil night environment to ease his frustrations.

The fall had smacked him back into reality, so he was now keenly aware of the walk ahead. His path crossed the dining hall and a few academic buildings, lit by streetlights so that students could find their way.

Now it seemed as though only every third street light was lit, casting unsatisfying patches of warm yellow glow onto the sidewalks. There were, as there always were, a handful of streetlights that shone a sanitary blue that cheapened the warmth of the other streetlights. He had noticed these lights before and had found the dissonance between the two colors oddly charming, but now, the sharp blue glared at him.

His gait was lazy with sleep, worsened by the empty stomach he had grown accustomed to during his long hours in the studio. The man took a turn with his path, now headed towards the stairs nestled between the dining hall and Barresi, and he felt the cold become freezing, walking against the strong wind. He thought back to the project he had spent so much of the day on. There was a particular sense of pride, the man thought, in categorically succeeding at such an unenjoyable assignment. He was eager for the critique.

A strong gust of wind nearly knocked him off his feet.

His attention snapped to just ten minutes before, when he had passed by a window through which he could see the workspace he had just left.

"I left the window open," he said, unaware of speaking out loud.

He turned on his heel and began to power walk back to the studio. Any concern for the path ahead of him, or for debilitating tiredness, was silenced. His paternal instincts for the project he worked so vigorously on forced one foot in front of the other.

Marching back, he felt the crunch of the snow under his feet but hardly knew he was walking. The blue lights now sickened him, and a thought in the back of his mind proposed that he could go a little slower, that a few minutes wouldn't make a difference. No matter. Fierce protection and copious self-directed rage had lit a flame in him to make sure he didn't let the excruciating day of work go to waste.

Accelerating, he thought about how little common sense one would need to possess to have closed that window. He crossed the road, vision blurred but not caring to look for cars anyway, turned down the sidewalk, and headed downhill towards the back door of the art building.

His focus zeroed in on the studio window around 20 feet ahead. His consciousness existed only in an all-white diorama where he saw his baby, a meticulously stacked pile of rings and blades of paper that gave the illusion of chaos. It was all white paper, but it had layers and intricacies that he felt gave it a cartoonish boldness.

He imagined the project as he might discover it, laying on the floor with a large segment disconnected from the rest.

He felt a force push him to the ground.

***

He awoke sometime later to the harsh light of the studio filtering through his eyelids, his body warring against the heat of his winter coat, which he still had on. He sat up on the concrete floor to shed the coat and check his phone. It was five o'clock AM.

Last night had been strange. It had felt surreal, like a dream, where everything happens before you can process it.

No.

He thought back, conjuring up specific details he had experienced last night: falling in the snow, the cold, the hunger.

Surreal, but real nonetheless.

He felt a breeze from the open window.

He whipped his head in the direction of the sculpture.

...It wasn't there.

Where it had stood remained the dolly he had borrowed from the ceramics division just in case the sculpture would need moving at any point. For somebody to have moved the life-sized work without the dolly made no sense.

He imagined, for a moment, how cathartic it would feel to get on his knees and slam his head into the concrete floor, given the emotional roller coaster this glorified wad of paper had subjected him to.

That was that.

The man stood up and, like a droid being assigned to a new mission, walked out, abandoning any thoughts of the sculpture. He still had time to sleep before class.

He shrugged his coat on as he stepped outside; it was as frigid as it had been before, but the air was now settled, peaceful. The sky was only slightly lighter than earlier. His body felt heavy.

He didn't particularly care what had happened to the sculpture. He had little appetite for speculation, and he could sense that he would never see the project again.

Even so, he wished for some logical explanation that he could relay to his professor. He winced to think of the palpable judgment that would be in the air when his classmates saw that he had only photos to show for the week's assignment.

He passed under the first of the few inexplicable blue streetlights on the path. He looked up. It felt like he had bonded with these streetlights during last night's walk.

The man finally approached the three-flight metal staircase that led uphill to his dorm. It looked unfinished, like the framework for a staircase rather than a staircase itself, and on the steps, there was a pattern of holes designed, he assumed, to allow precipitation to fall through. Still, the snow was high enough to completely cover a couple of steps at either end where the stairs met the ground.

Ascending, he chose not to think about the nauseating experience of being able to see through the surface he stood on, nor did it come to mind how unreliable his body and instincts were at this particular point in time.

Instead, he was disobeying his mind, thinking still of the paper sculpture that no longer sat waiting for him in Harder Hall. He felt something call him back to start over and enter the first critique with integrity, not having given up on the assignment. He reached the top of the staircase and gave himself an empty pat on the back.

***

The man stepped into his dorm.

The room was fairly organized, comfortable, and between his own art and the colorful tins and posters he had been collecting over the years, the room had a tasteful vibrancy of which he was proud.

As of late, though, the room had begun to betray the man's bad habits. The trash and recycling was overflowing, every surface but the bed was cluttered, and the floor was adorned with white splotches recording past battles between the slush and road salt he carried in on his shoes.

When he entered, the space called his attention to the chores that had needed completing for a while now; he hastened to a stack of colored notepads on the dresser to jot them down before allowing himself to take off his coat and mask.

Ignoring the complaints of his empty stomach, he collapsed into bed.

***

"What? I swear I had them; I don't know where they went." The man cringed at himself internally. The whole situation felt like a 90's horror movie trope, where a blonder-than-blond kid named Max can't get his parents to see that their new house is haunted.

But there was really nothing else to say. All he knew was that the sculpture and the photos had been there the night before. Now, looking at his phone, it appeared both were gone.

"Y'all can vouch for me that I was working on it yesterday, though, right?"

It was a small class, and so the classmates were indeed able to confirm his presence in the studio with a nod.

"Well, you don't have anything here for me to grade, so I'd suggest taking this next week to do another iteration. I'm willing to be lenient with the size of the project; I just want to see something completed."

The man felt like the embodiment of a sigh.

He sulked at his worktable for half an hour after critiques.

THE NIGHT SHIFT

KAITLIN "KATT" VILLANUEVA

GLASS. IT'S HARD for the mind not to construe odd visions from the bends in the light or hazy reflections. It's even harder when the mind dribbles off as you wait for a person to come in through the tall glass doors. While at work, I'm usually so caught up in homework that it's hard to force myself to sit attentively like the good check-in attendant I'm supposed to be. The sounds of the door swooshing open or feet echoing in the hollow entrance prompt me to perform my routine greeting: "Hello! Which studio are you going to? Did you do your health screening? Cool! Have a nice day!" When people leave, I watch them in the reflections of the door or the sheet of flimsy Plexiglas that encases me and the laptop. Though I'm usually absorbed in whatever laborious activity I must complete for class, I always make an effort to wish anyone who leaves a good day or night. Sometimes I get a mumbled return that doesn't sound much like anything, or I get nothing at all. Either way, I try to be kind.

The winter nights were approaching earlier, which meant all of my shifts would happen in complete darkness. The dull yellow street lamps do not provide much light, only enough to create confusing shadows from the trees. Other than them, it was up to me and the indoor fluorescent lights to ward off any spooky occurrences. One night, however, this did not stop those things from happening. Whether it was real or imaginary, I cannot shake what I saw out of my brain every time I come to work.

It had been a relatively early Tuesday shift, though it was pitch black out by 6 PM. Classes were canceled that day due to the treacherous winter weather, but the studios were still open for those who would rather work than enjoy a day off. As expected of tired college students, no one came in. Or at least, I don't think so. I was too caught up in my psychology reading to pay much attention to anything. With all of the readings, discussion posts, and lengthy lectures, my mind was spent, even though the week had hardly begun. I glued my eyes to my computer screen as I tried to make sense of the words in front of me, but my brain was gelatin.

Accepting defeat, I took my eyes from the screen and looked into the reflection of the Plexiglas where I saw a figure standing behind me. It was dark and limber. How long has he been standing there? Is he lost?

I turned around in confusion: nothing. Only the blank wall and directional signs were visible. My shifts were only an hour, so I knew that it was almost time to leave when I saw that the clock read 6:45. I put my laptop into my bag and prepared to wait out the rest of the shift. Though a bit confused by the odd figure I thought I'd seen, I didn't think too much into it.

But it wasn't long before I saw something again, and this time, it wasn't in the glass.

A pool of red was slowly creeping in my direction, almost like a snake winding its way through grass.

"Is a pipe leaking?"

It looked like blood, or some type of rusty slush. I sprung up from my chair to look around the rest of the lobby, but I saw no sign of anyone. I looked to my left and saw that the sludge was coming from a ceiling vent. By the time I pulled my phone out of my pocket to call a maintenance worker, the lake of red was gone. I thought someone must be trying to pull a prank on me. Thankfully, it had just struck 7, so I was able to get out of that total cheese feast. I came back to my desk and pushed the black rolling chair in before wiping everything down with a disinfectant wipe. I grabbed by bag and headed for the door, pulling on the cold metal handle.

No. You have to be kidding me. How was I locked in? Someone must really be pranking me, because this is just stupid.

"Bro, this isn't funny!" I shouted, glancing around the surrounding area. I banged on the door before remembering that there was an exit on the bottom floor where the Ceramics and Foundations studios were.

As I was making my way down, a loud bang stopped me in my tracks. I knew that I had to find out what was going on. If something was happening and I didn't stop it, I could lose my work study privileges. The hollow echo of the bang vibrated in my ears as I entered the main lobby. Like before, no one was there. I then decided to take a look in the bathrooms. Maybe someone fell or a pipe blew?

I was hesitant as I made my way to the dimly lit bathrooms. I checked the women's restroom first; though I was alone, I wasn't brave enough to explore the men's room yet. There might be things scarier than monsters and ghouls in there. I opened the heavy metal door and put my head through the crack. This restroom always gave me the creeps. Not only was it shady in the sense that it was poorly lit, but it always reminded me of something you'd see in horror movies. Who chooses to paint stalls red?

Aside from the odd decorative choices, I saw and heard no one. I crouched down to see if there were any pairs of feet in the stalls and saw none. Defeated, I closed the door and walked to the men's room. The door was already propped open, so I leaned my head in quickly to get a look.

Unlike the women's restroom, this one was lit a bit better and was surprisingly clean aside from the occasion sharpie drawings on the stalls and scraps of bathroom tissue on the floor. Again, I saw nothing.

When I turned to leave, the figure was standing only 15 feet away from me. I couldn't make out his face since it was a rule for us all to wear a mask at all times.

My voice quivered as I asked, "Can I help you, sir?"

A soft mutter came from behind his baby blue mask before he started to come closer. By this point, I could not suppress my fear, and I started to run in the opposite direction.

The squeak of my wet boots echoed through the lobby as I ran and hopped into the rickety elevator. Panicked, I repeatedly pushed the "close door" button.

It was too late.

The mysterious man stuck his hand in between the two doors as they began to close. I knew it. I was so dead. I can't run out of the elevator! Shit...I'm a goner. The doors, however, did not open, even with his hand in between them. The car began to lower as I watched his hand crush between the floor and the door. I let out a blood curdling scream, no pun intended, as his severed fingers rolled onto the floor of the elevator. I reached the bottom level and ran out, tears streaming from my eyes. I hoped someone else would be in the Ceramic or Foundations studios to help me, but all the spaces were vacant.

Getting no response to my cries for help, I ran into the nearest bathroom and locked myself into a stall. I clutched my knees to my chest as I sat on the toilet, trying to collect my thoughts and recount to myself what I saw. I knew I couldn't say in here long. I had to escape this nightmare.

Shit, the door!

I dashed out of the bathroom and towards the doors in between the two studio spaces. My arm reached out to the handle, pushing all of my weight on the door.

Just like the front door, this was locked too.

It wasn't long before I heard another loud bang.

My head snapped up. I looked around to see my roommate standing next to me at the check-in desk.

"Dude! It's 11 PM! Your shift ended hours ago! What're you still doing here?"

My heart started to relax as I realized I had fallen asleep at my desk. "Holy shit, man... I was having wicked dreams you won't believe."

"Well, tell me on the way home," she said. "It's starting to get bad out there."

I got up from the chair once again and performed the post shift rituals before leaving the desk. We both headed towards the door and I reached for the handle.

Locked.

Horror Class

Emily Swendson

"Good evening, class! My name is Professor Williamson, and welcome to The Horror Show! In this class, we will be analyzing horror and thriller movies before the year 2000 and then comparing them to horror and thriller movies after the year 2000. Each week, we will watch one old school and one new school movie, and you will have to discuss the differences in a one-page paper."

This class sounds easy. Watching two movies a week and only having a page to write is a piece of cake. Much easier than physics. I wonder what movies we will watch. Hopefully, none of the lame cheesy ones that are too predictable.

"On the syllabus, you will see that this week we are watching *Texas Chainsaw Massacre*, the 1974 original film, and comparing it to *Saw*, which was made in 2004."

Two of my favorite movies. This will be so easy to get done.

***

Two o'clock in the morning seems like the most appropriate time to construct a comparison between the two horror movies. Sleep evades me, so there's not a more suitable time to delve into the mysteries hidden in each film. Caffeine, the perfect additive to a sleepless brain, aids me as my fingers strike against the keys, barely keeping pace with the thoughts flowing through my head. The coffee fuels my brain and fingers but is failing to help my eyes. The longer I stare at the computer screen, the drier my eyes become and the heavier my lids feel. Drifting into unconsciousness, I can still feel my fingers typing and hear the clicking of the keys as they race to keep recording the thoughts.

Where am I? Why is it so dark? Did I fall asleep again? My roommate must have shut off my computer for me. I hope she made sure the work was saved this time before shutting it down. This is not right. Where is my bed? Where is the obnoxiously large window? Why are my wrists burning?

Looking towards my hands, they are not there; I can only feel them restrained to what I assume is a chair. My eyes are open, and darkness blinds me. A sack covers my head, restricting my air and making my head itch. I try to stand, but my bound legs cause me to slam back into the seat. I can hear blood whooshing in my ears, feel my heart trying to burst from my chest, hear the rush of the air through the sack trying to make it into and out of my lungs, feel the sack sticking to my face on every inhale, feel my chest heaving, feel my legs straining against the rope, and yet I can see nothing.

Thoughts race through my head, but I can't focus on one in particular. As I try to calm myself, I hear the distinct sound of water running through pipes. My breathing slows and my heart starts to settle. I must be in a basement. I rack my brain, trying to find a way out of this; I breathe slowly and take in as much air as the sack allows. The rope bites into the soft flesh of my wrists as I attempt to loosen its biting grip. I free my right hand first and rip the bag off my head. After my eyes adjust, I scan the room: there is a high window on the wall to my right, pipes that run all over the ceiling above me, and a staircase leading upwards on my left. Guess I was right about the pipes.

I look down and start untying my left hand when I notice the blood splatter around the chair. My eyes widen and my breath stops as panic settles in my gut. I do not want to die. My hand frantically tries to untie my other, and once they are both free, I reach down to try and get my legs loose. These ropes are much tighter than the ones my arms were bound with, and they rub my fingertips raw as I fiddle with them. I finally get both legs untied and just sit back in the chair to take a breath. Here are my options: I can use the chair, go through the window, and run into the night, not knowing where I am or where the nearest roadway is, or I can try the stairs and risk going through the door.

I am going for the window. I stand, carry the chair to the window and softly place it down. I carefully climb up, conscious of the noises I make. The window has a latch that is rusted and refuses to move. My fingers constantly slip off the partially broken latch as I yank on it, slicing them. Nice thing about adrenaline; blocks the pain.

The latch finally gives, and the window swings down at me. Flailing for the window, I reach to catch it before it slams against the wall. Luckily, my arms cushion the crash; unluckily, my arms will bruise. I clamber my way out of the window, finding myself using the ground as leverage to drag myself through. My pants and shirt snag on the edge, and I find myself on solid ground.

Just as I stand and begin looking around at my surroundings, a hand grabs my ankle and jerks me back towards the window. I scream, my heart racing as I crash onto the cold, damp ground. The arm continues yanking me backwards. My nails and fingers claw the ground, desperately trying to gain traction. The arm manages to drag me halfway back through the window as I continue to kick and scream, struggling and flailing, doing anything to break the arm's grip. I cannot get a hold on the ground and keep slipping backwards through the window. My hands grab onto the window frame to keep myself from going any further. I can feel the muscles in my arms straining to keep me free. I reach for the moonlight, reach for the trees, reach for the outside. My hands slip, and I fall through the window, back into the darkness of the basement.

Jolting awake, I realize I am in my dorm room. The light from my laptop blinds me. Shit. It was just a dream. No more late nights. As I return to finishing my essay, I notice what look like rope burns on my wrists.

96

Alfred Village, settled circa 1807.

The Village was originally called "Alfred Centre."

WALLED IN
JUNO TANGRY

I 'VE NEVER BEEN one for clichés, nor do I like when they provoke disbelief. But I sense things other people don't. That sounds silly, and even I have trouble believing it sometimes, but it's true. I hear footsteps creeping up the staircase and then back down, cabinet doors opening and closing, floorboards creaking all through the house. They used to bother me, and I used to fear whatever presence was in my home. Recently I've begun to accept that they occupied this house before me and unfortunately just got stuck. See, they're attached to this house and spend year after year repeating their final actions before death. Like a living person suffering from a mental or emotional trauma, they're reliving their worst moments, unable to move on. It's kind of sad, really, and I often find my mind wandering to what could have happened to them all. I try not to think about it.

My mind seems to get the better of me most often when my fiancé works overnights, as he seems to do more and more often these days, and I'm left to think about the hustle and bustle I hear in my empty house. I don't talk about this with him anymore, but I used to. As I told him the stories of the laughter echoing from the upstairs hallway, or the footsteps walking in endless circles in the living room, or the persistent cold spot in the upstairs bathroom, he would always twist his face into new expressions of disbelief. I'm afraid he thinks I'm crazy. I thought that maybe if I kept my stories to myself, his suspicion would subside. More and more he always seems all too prepared to go. I start to feel selfish, and I push these feelings away too. He always talks about his coworkers, and is often invited to the local bars after long shifts. I'm afraid he likes them better.

No, he's allowed to have friends. I don't like to control him.

When he's gone, I have a lot of time to myself. I'm a freelance writer between jobs, so I mostly work and fill out applications from home. My fiancé got a job offer last year, so about six months ago we relocated to this tiny rural town in the sticks some eighty miles from the nearest city. People from out of town only come here for the university nearby, as it's pretty much the only thing this town is known for. I considered applying, but I never got around to it. I'm not sure I'm cut out for collegiate life anyway. The people here are nice, somewhat standoffish, but I'm afraid they don't quite like newcomers. See, most of the residents have inherited their homes from parents or grandparents, and their families have lived in the area for generations. They don't seem to be warming up to us either, for we've yet to meet most of our neighbors on the street. If we see them out and about, they seem to avoid speaking to us and avert their eyes as we pass. I'm sure they're all nice people, so I shouldn't make assumptions.

We live in a rotting old farmhouse that my fiancé insists on fixing up. He says it'll be our big project, but I'm hesitant. He hardly finishes anything he starts, especially now. Even though I tried to explain that we don't have the money to fix what the house needs, he was too preoccupied with how low the selling price was to consider it. So I yielded. I didn't want to upset him. Living here now has made me wish I had pushed harder.

The wallpaper is peeling, the siding needs replacing, and the bathrooms have some of the worst water damage I've ever seen. It looks like the bathtub has been flooded, perhaps more than once, for the floor and lower walls are spotted and discolored. I can't forget about the kitchen; it's the most abhorrent room in the house if you ask me. It seems the last living occupants left in a hurry because when we arrived there were rats and ants crawling about, stealing the rotten food out of the pantry. The smell still hangs in the air when the windows stay closed for too long. The floor is uneven and the tiles have lifted, so they shift around as you walk. I avoid the kitchen as much as possible.

I sit alone in our bedroom, for it's the one room we've given the most attention. We hung thick curtains to distract from the warped, cloudy windows, as well as to suppress the awful draft they let in. The floor is neglected hardwood, and it too is warped and damaged, with large pits and digs in its surface. A crack flows down the wall behind the headboard, and I'm convinced it's getting bigger. It's often the subject of my nightmares in which I see it open up and swallow me whole. But I don't talk about that anymore either. We hung a painting over it. I try to keep an open mind, imagining the house's potential, and what it could look like after a significant amount of renovation. For now, I sit in our sunken old house and listen to my new roommates stumble about.

The footsteps I hear have been getting louder and more frequent. They seem more insistent, as if the walker is wearing heavy winter boots, and now it sounds as though they stop right outside the bedroom door and hover for a moment before continuing down the hall. The cupboards don't shut quietly anymore, but the doors slam shut against their frames. I've even noticed some of the knobs coming loose, though I can't be sure that's related. I haven't heard the laughter since the first time, and I'm not keen on hearing it again. The voice sounded like my sister, her infectious belly laugh she hates, and it took me a brief moment to register that she's not here. She has visited us only once since we moved, which she says is on account of her living so far away. I think she has something against my fiancé. I shouldn't say an awful thing like that, but sometimes I can't help it.

I try to tell myself that the laughter could have been anything, and that it's highly unlikely it was actually her voice, but it's never sat quite right with me. As these events continue getting louder and more frequent, I'm left to think about what they could mean. I imagine something is reaching out to me, as if it has something to say. I've often wanted to communicate with it, to see what it wants, but that sounds silly. My fiancé would have none of that; he's always been a skeptic. When we moved, I mentioned bringing my grandmother's deck of tarot cards, though I really didn't know how to use them, but he would hear none of it. He said he didn't want "crap like that in our house." So I left them with my mother, who has no doubt thrown them away by now. She's hardly a believer herself. I rarely ever think about the cards anymore, so they must not have been too important to me.

After a few days of relentlessly tossing and turning the idea in my head, I've decided I couldn't put off reaching out to whatever occupies my home, just to see what would happen. I try to convince myself that I won't find anything to prevent myself from feeling disappointed later. I have no idea how to start. I decide to do some research and see what I can find. After countless websites full of obviously fake ghost "encounters," I stumble upon a medium. Her page is full of language I can barely understand, and I quickly realize how much work I have to do.

***

I wring my hands as I pace the living room floor, boards creaking with each step. I haven't been this nervous in a long time. My fiancé is working; I didn't bother telling him I was bringing in a medium. I'm not sure what he would say if I did, and I'd like to keep it that way.

As soon as I hear the car in the driveway, I bolt to the door to greet her. A woman in her late sixties saunters toward the porch, bangles clanging on her thin wrists. She wears a long, flowing skirt of a silky material with dragonflies on it. Several necklaces of various lengths are shining and clicking together as she walks. I can't help but stare. Not to be rude, of course, but there is something magnetic and commanding about her presence, almost like she's supposed to be here. Before she even reaches the first step, she buckles forward and places a hand on her heart.

"Dear gods, you were right to contact me," she says with a solemn nod, her eyes wide and piercing. She slips past me and walks in. Stunned, I follow.

Gazing around the living room, peeking up the staircase, she seems to be searching for something. I offer her a glass of water or something to eat, but she seems to not hear me. Almost absently she walks from room to room, methodically exploring my house. She nods and mumbles to herself, like she's confirming a theory. The only thing I can do is wring my hands and follow her lead.

After fifteen minutes, she sits me down on the couch in the living room. "The presence in your home is a restless one," she whispers, "and I think you know it has been reaching out to you. Why are you afraid to answer?"

My mouth goes dry. How could she know that? I never told her I was afraid to answer.

"What do you mean, 'restless'?" My brow furrows. I try to stay skeptical.

"The spirit inhabiting this house is that of a young woman, murdered by her husband," she says with a wince, "and now she resides here, retracing her steps in life."

"But how can you know all that?" I reel back, processing her statement. "How do I know it's the truth?"

The medium smiles, nodding gently. "Let me show you."

She waves me over toward the kitchen, and I give her a hesitant look. We walk together past the threshold, and she is immediately drawn to the far wall. I stumble over the shifty tiles, embarrassed to let a guest see such a mess. She doesn't seem to notice it, however, and instead puts her ear to the wall, knocking on it with her fist. I try to ask what on earth she's doing, but she shushes me and keeps knocking. Before long, I hear a hollow "thunk" on the wall. I freeze.

"There's something in this wall," she says, continuing to knock, "and she wants you to know what it is."

"You can't be serious. How can you know there's something in there?"

"Believe me or don't, I just know what I'm told. In it lay her possessions, her life. It's the reason she can't move on." The medium sighs. It's like she can feel the spirit's emotions, or like she's affected by the supposed objects in the wall somehow. She takes several deep breaths before continuing. "She wants to speak with you. That's all I can hear now."

"Me? Why me? I hope I haven't upset her." I ball up the hem of my shirt in my hands, looking around the room as if I would be able to see her.

"Not at all. She only wants to communicate because she knows you will understand. This spirit reached out to the last occupants of this home, but they soon left after she made contact. I fear they had a similar dynamic to what she endured. All she wants is to speak to someone who will know how she felt here, what she went through." The medium resumes her solemn expression. "Someone who knows how love can hurt."

"I don't know what she means; my fiancé is good to me." I hurry through the words, trying to make myself believe them along with the medium.

All she can do is nod. "Well, I'd better get going. I'm not sure I can be of much more help here."

"What do you mean? We've only just started."

"She will reveal all to you. Will you answer her? It could mean the end of her suffering, and maybe yours as well." She picks up her coat and heads for the door. "Best of luck to you."

And with that, I stand alone in my living room once again. I'm not sure I'm ready to communicate with a spirit, and I certainly don't want to open up a hole in the wall for no good reason. But something about the medium's words grips me, and I can't get the idea out of my head. I think about it constantly until my fiancé arrives home, and I get so focused on the subject that during dinner, he prods me about what's distracting me. I tell him it's nothing, that I'm just tired, and he shrugs and leaves it alone. I decide to sleep on it and regroup in the morning.

**

3:00am shines brightly on the alarm clock when I hear a loud crash in the kitchen. I sit bolt upright, having been woken from deep sleep. My fiancé never wakes up during the night; I'm convinced he could sleep through anything. So it's up to me to investigate. Usually I would just ignore the sound and will myself to sleep again, but this time I feel something pushing me, compelling me to go. I get out of bed and tiptoe to the kitchen, turning the lights on as I do.

Once I get to the bottom of the stairs, I hesitate. It's probably nothing; I haven't heard anything since the first noise that woke me up. But I have to know. The medium's words fill my head again, and I force my feet to step forward. Before I reach the kitchen door, I notice a glass has fallen off the counter and shattered on the floor. This must have been what woke me up, and it brings a brief moment of relief before I realize that my fiancé has been asleep this whole time: neither of us could have knocked the glass over. I swallow hard, breathe deeply and push on into the kitchen. I'm disturbed to find that every cabinet door is wide open. My eyes widen and my hands grip the door frame tightly, the color draining from my knuckles. The air is thick and heavy, something I have never felt so strongly until now. I'm frozen for a moment, knowing that I'm the person that was meant to see this. I understand that this is a sign to listen to the medium and see what's in that wall. I step cautiously into the kitchen, glancing around at my open cabinets. One by one, I close them all as quietly as I can, but I'm not really sure why; maybe out of respect for the spirit. Then I rush to the wall.

I locate the hollow spot, and, without thinking, I thrust my fist through the wallpaper. It gives immediately, and I discover there's no drywall behind it. I'm welcomed by a small wooden box in an only slightly larger compartment. Its sides are decorated with an ornate, delicate pattern, blurred by its worn and degraded surface. A silver latch sits on its front, but it looks to be broken. I handle it gently and sit down on the floor to investigate it.

As soon as I open the lid, I feel a frigid breeze roll through the kitchen. The box's contents aren't anything particularly in-

teresting: family photos, children's drawings, and small trin-
kets. I manage to make out a name on one of the photographs:
Emelia Price. I sit back and think about what I can do with this
box. How can I return personal possessions to a dead person?

The only place I can think to go is the local cemetery. Realizing it's only three or four streets over heartens me. I assume
she'll be buried there, considering that the people here gener-
ally inherit their homes and thus live here most of their lives.
Before I have time to change my mind, I grab up the box and
a jacket from the hall closet and hurry out the door.

The air is freezing, so I walk fast. My mind races with
regret. Am I overreacting? Or just being silly? Maybe I should
just go back. I already put a hole in my kitchen wall, though,
and I'm carrying a box of someone else's precious belongings
to a cemetery. I've already come this far; I have to know if she's
really there. So I push on until I reach the grassy floor of the
cemetery, where I scour the stones to find someone named
Price.

I locate an Edward Price, the name, along with the word
"husband," etched onto an intricately crafted marble head-
stone with a small bird carved on its front. I look among his
neighbors. On the surface of the closest stone, a rough, flat
one sitting very close to the ground, I see a poorly executed
"Emelia" with "wife" underneath. I want to cry as I compare
the two headstones; I can finally see the extent of her mistreat-
ment. I decide to leave the box next to her name, patting it
gently. In time, I find myself sitting by the grave on a small
bench, not thinking about anything in particular. I figure that
after all this time, Emelia needs a friend. Maybe that's a silly
thing to say, but it comforts me.

I must have sat in the cemetery for quite some time because the sun begins to hit my back as I walk home. I hadn't

thought to return before my fiancé woke up. I open the door to find him dressed for work, fuming.

"Where have you been?" He stomps through the living room toward me, his eyebrows raised sharply. "And could you please explain the hole in the wall?"

"You wouldn't believe me if I told you."

"I already can't believe you! After all of your talk about ghosts and bumps in the night, and now *this*? I should have you committed." He's practically spitting the words at me.

"Yeah, maybe that would shut me up," I retort without thinking. I never speak to him like that. Worried, I look up to find him growing even angrier.

"What did you just say to me?" He steps closer, now almost in my face. "You don't talk to me like that." He looks like he could hit me.

I take a deep, long breath. "Get out."

"Excuse me?"

"You heard me. I want you out. We're done."

"You are *not* breaking up with me over this. You're being ridiculous. Do you realize how irrational you sound?"

"I am making perfect sense. You have work soon; you should go. By the time you come back the locks will be changed, so I suggest finding a place to stay." I stare him in the face. I feel an overwhelming sense of calmness, not the urge to run away like I usually do when we fight. I feel this calm despite having no idea how to change the locks, but I assure myself I can figure it out.

"I can't believe this," my ex-fiancé shouts as he reaches for his coat. "You're fucking crazy. Do you really think you'll be able to afford this place on your own?" He wants to say more, but checks the time and realizes he's late. He throws curses and insults as he walks through the front door, punctuating his exit with a loud slam.

I stand alone in my house, as I have become well-accustomed to, and this time it feels different. I said exactly what I wanted to, did exactly what I thought was right, and I know Emelia can finally be at peace after what happened last night. And for the first time in a very long time, I feel peaceful too. I can't help but smile, both with pride and relief. Laughter soon overtakes me, and tears well up as I look forward to my newfound freedom, as well as Emelia's. I laugh to myself in my living room, having never felt better.

Alfred's donation stand, located on University Street.

THE DONATION
JOSIE FASOLINO

SINCE MOVING TO Alfred, I've learned there are very few things to keep myself occupied. It's quiet, the winters are numbingly frigid, and most shopkeepers burrow into their homes for the weekends. The town appears vacant, and I have not heard so much as a whisper from my neighbors or a creak of a door since situating myself in the Brick. I have found myself in a routine of visiting the local donation spot down near Main Street, as I can't resist the free knick-knacks and treasures.

On the top shelf lie small plush bears and vintage glassware, while boxes of old cards, floral stickers and books topple onto one another at the base. Just yesterday, I perused the selection and found two mismatched earrings with dangling charms and beads, and a box full of yarn and needles. How perfect for an art student like me! And guess what's even better? I have finally met someone else who lives in this ghost town. I go each and every day, just a quarter past two, and normally, I'm left alone long enough to read a whole book right then and there. However, just a few weeks ago, I walked down the street and saw a small, elderly woman staring at the layers of magazines someone had just put out. We glanced at each other quickly, but I didn't say hello. I turned around and scurried back up the street, not knowing why I left so suddenly. I think I was just nervous, since I am not the best at socializing, especially with strangers.

The second time we crossed paths, I forced my lips to curl upward in a somewhat friendly manner. She didn't seem to take much notice of me, but she returned the smile back. I wonder if she's a local here? She did not appear outwardly strange, but her smile did seem a bit off. Her lips looked as if they were receding inward. Maybe it's just aging? We stood next to each other for a few minutes more, and then I left.

At the third interaction, however, I forced myself to make some type of introduction. Isn't it too peculiar that we had met three times in a row at the same time of day? I picked up an old illustrated medical book on mouth diseases and dental hygiene, and I carefully flipped through the pages. This would be a perfect book for a collage.

"Aren't these older illustrations remarkable?" I asked the woman.

She turned toward me and nodded shyly. Since that encounter, we have met at the stand several times, and I find her presence to be rather comforting now. She doesn't speak or make gestures or bombard me with questions, but simply appears to enjoy my company, as I do hers. She only reacts with that queer, peculiar smile as she watches me explore. I don't pay much attention to her expression though, assuming she is just anti-social like I am. She also never seems to take anything from the stand, which I find a bit unusual. Maybe she finds pleasure in taking a walk down here to the donation stand, watching others stop and go as they ponder and collect. I sift through bags of toys and stacks of CDs and arrangements of fake plastic flowers while she stands there, quietly watching my treasure hunt. I've started to wonder if she's looking for something specific that has yet to pop up here at the stand.

***

I think I'll go to the stand again tonight. I have some empty notebooks and old white beads from a class project. The weather is rather unpleasant. Most sounds are drowned out by the wind pushing through the trees and the occasional car tires screeching on the slippery roads. The falling snow is soft and bright, but it completely consumes the air, limiting my vision. As I approach the stand, I see a blurred figure. I'm close enough now to recognize that small frame: the elderly woman. Why is she out on such a terrible night? It's freezing, and the streets are dangerous for unstable legs. I'm closer now, and I give her a small nod before opening my bag. I want to do this quickly and get out of here; it's getting late. I try arranging the notebooks neatly in the corner, but my glasses are fogging up. The wind is blowing my hair in every direction, and I can't hear anything very well. I'm trying to find a spot for the beads so they won't roll away.

"T-tttt."

What was that? I glance to the right, and the old woman's rounded, wrinkled face looks distorted. Her eyes bulge from the sockets, and her lips are pursed. She looks crazed, mumbling to herself while trying to look over my shoulder and see my hands.

"Tee. Tee."

"What is it? I can't hear you."

Her mouth is barely open, but she's trying to say something. She's kind of scaring me. I've never heard her voice before; it sounds muffled and nasally. Maybe she's just out of it? I really don't know. I need to leave. She just took a step closer to me—I accidentally slip, scattering the beads in the snow. Now she's bent down, shaking her head aggressively.

"Teeth."

Teeth? Did she just say teeth? She's scratching at the snow, trying to find the beads as I back away slowly. Should I run? Is she crazed? She picks up one of the beads and stares at it for a moment, cupping it in her hand. She brings her face down to her hand and whispers something I cannot make out. She rises, places it in my hand and walks away, fading into the snowy blizzard. I run back up the street, confused and cold, unsure of what to say or do.

It's been several days since that incident, and I haven't seen the woman since. Maybe she was just delirious from the weather so she mistook my beads for teeth. I've had so many assignments to do and so little sleep that I'm sure I could have just imagined it. I was going to throw away the bead she gave me, but I keep rolling it between my pointer and thumb in my pocket, rubbing over its smooth outer surface.

***

I thought I'd get over that strange night, but I can't stop thinking of that woman. Why did she want teeth so badly? Or did she think I killed someone and pulled out their teeth? No, no. What is wrong with me? She probably just lost her dentures or something. I really have no clue, but I can't get the thought out of my head. I feel like I'm going crazy. All I do now is sit and stare at the bead and think of teeth.

What about them intrigues me? They're round and sometimes pointy on the ends. They can be sharp and bumpy and smooth and matte and shiny. Teeth are so nice, I wish I still had them...wait. Why did I just think that? I have all of my teeth.

***

Hm, I'm pretty hungry. I'll grab a grilled cheese and tomato soup at Powell.

"This is delicious. If only I had—"

"I need teeth. Help me, please. I need them. I'm deformed, I'm hideous, please, your teeth. They're all I need."

What, where did that come from? Was that from my head? That sounded like the old woman. I don't see her anywhere, though. Am I hearing things? I need more sleep. I wonder how she is doing. She must have been lost and confused that night. I feel bad that I didn't help her.

***

God, teeth-this, teeth-that. I keep hearing voices in my head telling me about teeth. What is happening to me? I don't know what to do. Who needs teeth? All I can think about is that old woman. Is she ill? Maybe she's not doing well. What if she's hurt and she was trying to tell me something?

***

Gosh, it really is cold tonight; the winters are brutal in Alfred. Whoa, I see her. She's by the stand again! Why is she here? I need to make sure she's okay. I take a few steps toward her, leaving enough room for me to escape if need be. She stands there quietly for a few moments, not acknowledging my presence in the slightest. Then she turns and offers me that same eerie smile she always does.

"I don't know your name or where you live, but we have met several times," I say. "Are you okay? Last time we met you were talking about teeth. If you need help, I can try to be of assistance."

She says nothing and continues to smile at me. I thought she was really sweet, but her body and facial expressions give me the creeps. Something about her is off; I still want to make sure she's okay, though.

"Listen, I'm here to help. If teeth are what you're looking for—"

"Ye-yes, teeth," she says while slowly inching closer to me. "I need teeth, please. Won't you help me?"

"Did you lose your dentures, ma'am? I don't understand you." The woman creeps up close to me, opens her mouth wide and flashes her gums at me.

"Look, look. Teeth, I need teeth, please help me, please, won't you give me teeth?"

Nothing remains except dark bumps, oozing with puss and blood. Her teeth are gone and her tongue is rotting away into a pale pink, greenish lump of flesh. The smell of her breath is rancid as if she's been eating spoiled milk and fecal matter. I feel sick, oh god. Wait, what is that white shape there? Is it one tooth? I lean closer. No, it's moving; it can't be a tooth. Wait— there are more, and they're twisting and turning and sliding around in her gums.

They're maggots.

I back away and keel over, fearing that I may puke in front of her. My head is spinning and my vision is going blurry. I feel my body give out, and everything goes black.

***

Wait, was that real? No, no, it must have been a dream. It couldn't have been real. I feel like I'm losing my mind.

***

It must have been real; I saw those maggots move with my own eyes. She needs my help, doesn't she? I don't know what to do. Teeth. Teeth. Teeth. Where do I get them? That poor, sickly woman. I can't stop thinking of her and her rotting gums. She needs my help. What do I do? Sh-should I give her mine? I don't know how much I need them. I'm young, and I can get them fixed and replaced. She is going to die: she needs my help. Okay, I think this is the most logical decision, right? It's my only option. I have to. I rush over to my utility box, scrambling through the glue and extra blades. There, waiting, are my pliers. They'll do. My fingers make their way to the back of my mouth, gliding along the small bumps and ridges of each individual tooth. The pliers are not too large, so they fit well into the small gaps between my teeth. During the first yank, I feel quite a bit of pressure, but not much pain. I position my arm on the table, give a quick twist, and rip up. It worked! It really worked. My molar falls to the ground along with a stream of blood and saliva. The pain is only starting to hit me now. My mouth is becoming sore all over, and the back of my mouth is numb.

Pull, twist, yank.

Pull, twist, yank.

Pull, twist, yank.

Over and over and over, till I'm left with no more. I've done it; now I can donate my teeth to the old woman. I don't feel so good though. I think I might lie down for a while. My vision is getting hazy and I can't feel my body. I try to talk, but I can no longer feel my lips or tongue.

***

Whoa, I guess I've been asleep for a while. Where am I? Am I in the hospital? The whole room is white and smells of chemicals and a young woman is standing next to me checking my temperature.

"Hello miss, this young woman said she found you passed out near the donation stand on Main Street. You had a pair of pliers by your side and were covered in blood and your own teeth. I know this must be a lot to take in, and you can't talk well right now, but do you know who did this to you?"

"W-well yes, of course I do." I can barely speak. My mouth is throbbing. "I-I did it for the old woman. She needed my help, yo-you see. She told me this ghastly story of how she got very sick and developed a severely sore throat." Ugh, the blood is coating my own throat as I speak. I can feel it dripping down my esophagus. I need to tell this nurse the story, though. "H-her entire mouth became swollen and she lost the ability to eat solid foods and talk normally. Her mouth was so diseased—" I hack out a few coughs— "—that her teeth began to rot away! Ho-horrible, isn't it? She was in such pain and was ashamed of her appearance, I swear to you!" I need to spit this blood out, but I don't want the woman to leave. She'll call the other nurses. I'll just swallow the blood. "All s-she wanted was a new set of teeth. How could I not help her? She was so k-kind to me, always meeting with me at the same time every day to watch me peruse the stand. I think she was hoping someone would be kind enough to donate an old set of dentures or some spare animal teeth. She just wanted to feel normal again. Anyway, I'm fine." I cough again. "I can get replacements, no worries. Have you seen her? When will she pick up my teeth?"

***

Weeks have passed, and I haven't seen the old woman. It's hard to accept that none of this was real, but my therapist has been helping me. Maybe I was just scared of living in a new place, and I made the old woman up in my head. That's entirely possible! I'm always tired and stressed, so I may have just imagined it. My mouth has been slowly healing, and I will be able to get a pair of dentures in the following weeks. I'm so confused by my actions, and I wonder if I really did go insane. Why would I have pulled my own teeth out? That was so stupid and scary of me. I've never heard of anyone doing that. Anyway, I think I need to cheer myself up. There's no point in getting mad about it now. Maybe I'll go to the donation spot again, just to find some fun little treasures. I won't stay long because my therapist told me not to go there anymore.

***

There's some fun stuff today. Old sheet music, fashion magazines…ooh! A hand thrown ceramic mug, how pretty. I could totally use this. Some old photos? Interesting, I don't see people throw these out a lot. There are too many to look through now, so I'll just take a handful and look at them at home. I bet these will be great for collaging.

***

I found some cool stuff today! I'm really feeling better now. Man, that donation spot always helps me relax. I got this cool LIFE magazine and some stickers for my collage, and ooh, I got those old photographs. I should check them out. This first one's cute, it's an old couple. On the back it says, "Birdie and Mark in Summer, 1916." How sweet, I love her outfit. This next one is of a small child with overalls riding on a bike. On the back it reads, "Joey's first bike ride, 1914." Huh, this other one looks kind of gloomy. It's a bunch of people in hospital beds with nurses running around. The space looks familiar. In the center is an old woman, sitting up in her bed.

I flip over the photograph and read out loud, "Sylvia's first attempt at smiling without teeth, the toll of the Spanish Flu, the Brick, Alfred, 1918."

THE VILLAGE HOUSE
S. K. SAGE

Nothing about this feels real.
It is just a haze, just a haze.
The steps I take are as honest as those in a dream.
But where am I?
Where am I?
Because I am not here,
*   I am not here.*

THE HOUSE THAT rests on sprawling South Main Street had once been called Alcott, but only ghosts now live to remember it as such. The Alcott it had been named for was long dead.

It is for this reason that I do not hold a singular hope that its name shall ever be said again. Of this I am certain, and more, for not even my own name shall be etched *in memoriam* upon a gravestone.

It was the early summer of 1918 when I received the letter.

From it, I had learned of my father's passing in Rochester, and that I now would inherit all his possessions and obligations, all of which were rooted firmly in a small town near the Pennsylvania border. There had been no tact when speaking on these matters, and one must believe that the war and influenza of this year had washed much of the sugar from our words.

It was at this time that I found myself aboard the Erie. Far from the rigid comforts of the Stone School where I had spent much of my life in study and practice, I traveled ever north-westerly to the small village called Alfred.

Alfred seemed to belong in a dream of mine, my time there spent at the whims of a drunken haze. This blurred exis-tence had haunted me in Cornwall-on-Hudson as it remains to haunt me now.

I was only a small child when I had left, but it seemed this wooded memory became more tangible as from train to Red Bus I went—purely by the generosity of the other men in Al-fred—watching as the clanging Station became the humble Village.

In specific, I was greeted by the quiet Main Street, where the summer air brought with it the smells of stables and un-dergrowth. The village was just as empty as the cities I knew. Summer and war called upon many young men and women, of which this collegiate land had many to spare. They were in high demand in these sickened times.

The address to the Alcott house was written in the letter, but I found I did not need it. My feet blindly carried me past storefronts and homely windows, wooded lots and skeletal foundations.

Alcott had been a gift from the patriarch to his young bride. Christened in 1900, the final touches put to its body, it was to become my childhood home on which I could look back with fondness, where his bride would spend her summers when I had grown.

A plan blinded by love that, it seemed, God had no inten-tion of allowing.

As a new owner, it would have been easy to view the house with a distant attitude, an objective eye. However, its looming, weathered redness welcomed me, a prodigal son in the embrace of his family, with open arms. I could not refuse such a homecoming, but it felt strange in the deepest recesses of my mind and heart.

It was not lost to me that this must be some hardy Fate's cord for me to inherit Alcott now. At twenty years old, I was the same age as my father was when he had gifted this house to my mother.

And now here I was to take his place in this village, lost to the woods and time.

***

Alcott was a modest house unfit for a family larger than mine, but it would pose no issue for a young bachelor. The swing of the front door revealed a well-groomed interior. It had been under the care of the obsessive patriarch, and as such, it looked as if it had not been lived in for some time. Yet, it had to have been, for it was not so long ago that his body stood here—before he found sanctuary in his last days in the Flower City.

I admired the multitudes of paintings upon the walls, which left hardly a space for the wallpaper to leech through. Each depicted the locale, or similar bucolic landscapes, reminding me that there was more to the thickets and hills than crumbling farmhouses and dirt-dust roads.

As I looked, I thought the lack of photographs was odd. I could not recall much of my young life, but I could remember having my boyhood visage captured. Not one photograph hung from a peg, nor sat upon a slim shelf. These black, white, and sepia memories were misplaced, or lost with a purpose to hide the story of the patriarch and his family.

As distracting a finding as this was, I had neither the energy nor present interest in searching for what my father had decided was unworthy of the house. The stairs called out to me, my luggage weighing heavy in my hands, and I walked to the foot of them. In the process, I felt a sensation I can only describe as…

Look at me, look for me.

Turning my head, my gaze rested uneasily upon a white door to my right. Latched with a thin metal bar, the basement waited patiently behind it.

I had no desire to look inside, no matter how briefly, and promptly turned my back to it and began my ascent to the bedrooms.

These bedrooms, of which there were four, were closed.

To the far right, I recalled vaguely from my memory, was the master bedroom. The unspoken rite that the owner must rest his head there floated through my mind, and it was here, as I wavered at the top of the stair, that I again felt discomfort within Alcott.

I walked to the door, my hand shocked by the static of the handle, and my shoes clicked against the threshold. The combination became a flashbulb bursting upon a deeply harbored memory. Caught in a trance, I could see my boy-self visiting my mother's sickbed.

I was so, so young, and as such the memory was lost in Fauvism ideals. As disorienting and confusing as it was, I could see the young son rush upon his mother's bedside. I could feel the feverish warmth as they sat, cheek-to-cheek, before he slid comfortably onto her shoulder.

Only that, before it fell back to shadow, and all I saw and felt before me was disconcertion.

I placed my bags at the doorway, having no intention of stepping into the room, much less sleeping there tonight. I did not need further memories.

Attempting to distract myself, I moved to open each door on the second floor.   One room at the landing of the stair coaxed me to look in. The color and the decor of the room immediately marked it as mine. However, it was devoid of childness; the bed was too big for a youth, and there was nothing belonging to a boy within.

It did not surprise me that the patriarch had scrubbed the stain of his child from the house's memory, while I resided hundreds of miles away without a functioning nor happy recollection of this place. Neither was the house surprised, perhaps, and it was a mercy for my existence to be ripped from it.

But I was here now. I was here.

Pulling myself from melancholy thoughts, I heard a sound that seemed ill-fitting for where it echoed from.

Tet, tet, tet...

Hazarding a guess that the floorboards were the source of the sound, I stood still, but the noise continued. My attention was fixed upon a closet, shuttered closed, on the far wall. There should have been nothing within it.

Tet, tet, tet...

I crept to the closet door; my fingers pressed tentatively against the white-wood shutters. The sound was from here, but no wind was its conductor. No object within was its orchestra. If it was a rat or similar pest, then so be it.

I pulled open the door, and...my eyes rested upon nothing.

Or, rather, a visible nothing.

The noise had ceased, but what it left behind felt odd, as if I were blind and someone stood in front of me. Fueled by electric apprehension, I shut the closet and fled the second floor in favor of greener pastures.

***

The yard was of clover and clumps of lush grass, breaking against the edge of the woods that threatened to swallow this village.

I could see, in the distance by the edge, specks of bees dancing around the small flowers and weeds. Despite the delicate image, I would not go much further than where I presently stood for two reasons, primarily being that within the woods, beside the shallow creek that runs through it, lay the buried mother, as I had been told by my father. He had expressed fear that I should become sick from her corrupted body, so I had never been to the grave, but I had watched.

The second reason was that my attention was suddenly caught on a crudely built doghouse to my right, scarred by the seasons and bearing no canine within. Small cobwebs peeked out from the opening of the mud-and-moss brown doghouse. On the ground, crumbling from the weather, were the leather scraps of a leash. Specks of it covered my hands like ash as I searched for some etched or written name of the creature, some explanation for the leash's presence.

I could not recall ever owning a dog.

Any further reasoning brought about only more questions, of which no answers materialized out of the mildewed wood. The scraps became a fidget plaything in my hands as I stared at the doghouse.

Abruptly, a rattling bark pained my ears and sent me stumbling back onto the grass. My eyes screwed shut in expectation of the thing jumping from the shadows of the shallow house and onto my beating chest.

But I did not feel its weight against me, and I soon opened my eyes to see nothing.

My back stained by the lawn, I was left in the resulting silence, clinging to the leash like a rosary until I could breathe without a sour shudder.

***

It was early evening; the sun had not yet set, but the gray had begun to settle into the bright sky when I nervously re-entered Alcott and decided to entertain myself by making dinner. The kitchen presides in the far back of the house, in its own nook, overlooking the yard. Despite the doghouse sitting just a few feet from the window, the busywork of cooking helped me to not dwell too long on it.

It did not last, however.

As the pot simmered, a knocking sounded on the front door. Hurried politeness echoed in the fist falls, and while I am not usually one for answering at this hour, the calmness of Alfred persuaded me to check on the person.

I begged their pardon as I opened the door, my civil glance falling upon a man pressed close to the threshold. I took a step back, out of instinct, as I tried to take in his whole image.

His hat was tipped, the shadow of its brim obscuring the left side of his face. Although mysterious, he looked pleasant enough. He appeared to be young, not much older than myself, and he had a sort of hesitant gleam in his eye. He held a small suitcase in his hands. In the gray light it was hard to see much else.

"Good evening," I said.

The man stared at me curiously. I did not really know why; perhaps it was because I had un-subtly positioned myself as if I were a brace upon the door.

"Evening," he replied at last. "I had an accident up the hill. I was wondering if I could get my bearings here before heading into town."

The request seemed peculiar to me, for reasons spanning from my own disinterest to the illogical request of seeking temporary refuge here. However, I could tell from his eyes that he was rather shaken, and it would have felt contrary to the values of Alfred to force the man to walk much further down darkened South Main Street without, at least, a glass of water.

I allowed him in.

Telling him I would return with some minor food and drink, I asked if he would wait in the living room. As I left, the click of his shoe heels against the wooden floor grew quieter.

Alcott was small, and so I had no qualms about leaving him to his own devices for a moment or two while I played host. I would hear everything, I thought, but as I clicked off the stove, all sound ceased.

Fearing some invader travesty, I hastily grabbed a glass of water and plastered a smile onto my face before rushing back to him.

And, as both glass and smile had been brought together, so too did they shatter upon the floor in sharp, shining pieces.

The man was not there.

I darted throughout the house in search. He could not have simply vanished into thin air, no, and so I opened doors and peered in corners like some mismatched game of hide-and-seek.

"Please, there's no need to hide," I said quietly. "Whatever happened, I…"

I did not know how to finish the sentence. My sympathy, driven out of propriety and fear, could only make so many appeals before they became unkeepable promises, and so I let the words die on my lips.

I walked every inch of the interior of Alcott, waiting to hear the man giggle like a schoolboy or rush at me with the violence of a criminal. I would have liked either to have happened, because the alternative, the truth in this case, was far more disturbing to me.

He had vanished without a trace.

***

The sun had finally set, the gray twilight seeping into the house like smoke. Alcott was not wired well for lighting, and so gas lamps glowed subtly against the growing darkness.

I was unsure if I would ever sleep, my body wracked with nervous and restless motions that carried me left-right-right-left across the house until every atom of it was covered in exhaustive footprints. As I paced, I winced at every click and creak, my head shooting in the direction of the noise like some startled deer before realizing the sound was my own.

There was no ease in this house, and that bad feeling grabbed at my clothes and skin like a frightened child. That simile is apt, I think, for I felt no malignity even now. It was mournful and despondent. It demanded to be felt, but not as risk of punishment.

I wanted to leave this place and sell it to whomever, but though the paperwork would have to wait until morning, it would not take long for me to evacuate and forget about Alcott.

The thoughts I had were accompanied by the metronome sound of my walking until a new sound overtook my own.

Running.

Above me, frantic pounding against the wood floor caused dust to fall from the ceiling. I had no earthly idea how I had not come upon the runner in my search.

Frozen, as if a victim of Medusa, I listened. From the far left: going, going, until they fell quiet in the master bedroom.

I waited for a long, long time before I had the where-withal to move from the first floor, past the railing, up to the blind corner where the master bedroom resided. I would have jumped at the sound of a falling needle, but the house seemed to settle, and I convinced myself that there was no one.

Disoriented and weary, I found a sliver of humor in being toyed with by revenants that wished no more credence to their existence than whatever my fogged mind could produce.

***

My mind soon forced upon me the idea of sleep. Be-gone, the disturbance of the ghosts that wormed their way in through the spaces of bricks; I must rest if I am to stay sane.

I began my retirement, turning off the lights and making sure everything was locked, which, I must tell you, I did with a deep earnestness. When done, I started to ascend the stairs, though I felt disquieted as I went.

As if a nest of spiders had broken upon me, creeping up my back, I thought I could feel something following me up the stairs. I feared to look behind me, afraid that a hanged thing with a rigor mortis grin would be staring back. It was such a childish imagining, and equally childish was my worry that the basement door had somehow opened.

This feeling propelled me up the stairs. When I felt the Hanged Man's gnarled hand brushing my shirt, I pushed myself into the nearest room and slammed the door closed in nightmare exhilaration.

My back rested against the carved wood, my chest heaving with devilish butterflies that reminded me I was a breathing thing.

I locked the door and, when the adrenaline faded, I could see that I had thrust myself into my childhood room. The boyhood colors gave me a sense of comfort, almost encouraging me to tuck my head under the covers to protect myself from any gallows creature.

I must tell you that I do not recall undressing or falling asleep, but I remember being tormented by dreams, or perhaps memories; I cannot say. But they were a confounding narrative that not even the Pythia or her patron could delineate.

***

When I awoke, I found myself twisted in bedsheets. Shackled in cloth, I sat up, bleary-eyed, to free myself.

And that was when I heard it. Again, again, again.

I must have resembled a re-animated cadaver: half-slumped, risen with his arms outstretched to his legs with a look of morbid curiosity flashing in his eyes.

What sounded like footsteps echoed above my head, and I realized, as dust began to fall about me, that it came from the attic. I had not yet found the entrance to that room, even in my anxious state last night, and yet, the sound was as clear as if I were the one walking above.

My hands, temporarily frozen in uncertainty, now worked quickly to untether myself. I soon slid from the bed quietly, willing away any noise my steps could make with the confidence of a dormouse. I did not know from where this brazenness came, as I still hoped to grab my luggage and take the earliest train to some other cursed part of New York.

Nevertheless, I moved ever closer to the door. Still, the steps continued.

I listened to the noise, perched. Then, as if I could be heard, the steps moved away from my head and grew slightly quieter. I followed the noise and stopped in front of the closet.

I could almost hear the tapping of yesterday as I crept, in ghostly reprisal, to the shuttered thing. I opened the door once more, searching in the dim light until I found the faint paint-slit outline of the attic door. The attic was so discretely made that it seemed impossible for anyone to find it.

No string hung down to give it away, and even when I pushed the cut segment of ceiling up, no stair revealed itself. There were shelves that lined the wall of the closet, and I used them to my advantage. Like an insect, I crawled up into the musty space where I was welcomed with sudden silence.

Daylight had begun to stream in through the window, enough for me to see, but to see what, I had no idea.

There were scarce boxes here. When one has a basement cellar, what need is there to have memories kept above? And given the odd location of this attic entrance, I was unsure how helpful it would even be to hold anything here.

I hesitated at one of the boxes, an automatic and unconscious decision. I knelt, the dust coloring my knees, and tore open the box.

Inside, by the hazy light, I could see picture frames. I lifted out each heavy frame, the photographs gleaming from anti-exposure, with the care of an archaeologist in an ancient land. Through the black, white, and sepia, I gazed upon the youthful face of my mother.

In all my memories, though they were few, this was perhaps the first time I had actually seen her face: the quirk of her lips, the shimmer in her eyes, the girlish attitude that painted her womanly look; the way she was possessive of me, the way she leaned against my father.

Each image of her as healthy and beautiful as the last, I would not have been able to tell you she would suffer and die at the hands of a festering illness.

And as my fingers traced the shattered memories, I heard creaking stairs.

The idea of the spectral intruders quickly returned to me, and I could not believe I had forgotten them, so entranced had I been by the Siren's promise of tangible memories.

I dropped from the attic, pressing against the bedroom door as I listened to the shifting outside.

It did not take long for the sound to go silent, and I tentatively unlocked the door to peer into the hallway. All my suppressed fear was made sudden horror as I saw that the basement door stood open. The fractal fingertips of the cellar darkness clutched at the white painted door frame.

I descended the staircase and stopped short of the door in reverent awe. A phantom hand reached out and intertwined with the dark fingertips, pulling the door open to expose it to the morning.

Perhaps the hand had been mine—it must have been, given the proximity—but I cannot recall.

With each step into the basement, the echo of flesh against stone sounded out the years. Had I never awoken from my dream?

When my soles rested on level ground, I faltered. I did not know if it was the airless scent of the place, or the sudden weight upon my shoulders.

It is such a funny thing, memory. I remember only fragments, as if I were relaying what I had seen long ago upon a stage. As I stood in the concrete cellar, it was just the same feeling.

Some involuntary thought wormed its way into my mind, that of me in the body of the patriarch as I walked across the cold, gray floor. It was not something from my own thoughts that I followed, but something blindly projected onto me. Like Theseus with his lady Ariadne's thread, I traced my way through the shelves and crates, taking steps to find where I was meant to go, and soon, resting at my feet was a small valise. It looked painfully familiar, and as I crouched to look at it, I knew why.

Undoing its latches, I retrieved a passport that sat graciously atop the items within. The name of the owner, finally known to me, was Thomas Nesbith.

His picture was an unassuming portrait of the vanished man.

I had closed everything up again, a sick feeling in my stomach, when I heard the basement door close with a perturbing *thud*.

Jumping to my feet, I dashed up the shallow steps and banged my fists against the door. I would have screamed to whoever had done this, but I knew it was hopeless. That realization came out of me in the form of a mirthless laugh, my head resting against the door in an exasperated surrender.

I could sense movement behind me, and I spoke blindly to it, "What is it? Hm?"

As if its silence were answer enough, I opened my eyes and lolled my head to the side in annoyed fatigue.

"Content enough in playing such games with me? Making me the Fool?"

My peripheral vision caught a glimpse of who stood beyond me, and I felt the pulsing memories again. As palpable as the dust in my lungs, the mirage of a fever emanated from the figure.

Matron Alcott, the hem of her nightgown floating ever slightly above the floor, stood gracefully, as if she were accompanied by angels. However, that was not the only feeling that she projected. The other, more sinister, grabbed at my shirt and would have forced me to my knees were they not locked in fearful recognition.

I was her son, but I felt like nothing more than a trespasser at that moment.

Pulled by some holy binding, I found myself moving closer, closer, until I stood a breath away from her.

"Mother…"

Her face softened at the acknowledgement, as if she had waited an eternity to hear me say the word. The solemnity of the action was only marred by her appearance, for she did not resemble her photographs. She looked ghastly, gaunt as the plague itself.

She parted her lips to speak, pushing her vocal cords, but all that it brought forth was black bile that spilled from her withered lips like tar onto the frills of her neckline, and down, down. I could see the stains that prior efforts had left upon the soft nightgown.

"What is this?" Pity and disgust filled my chest. "Who did this?"

As if she knew I pursued a medical practice, she extended her arm to me, and I took the frail thing in my hands. Even with her ghostly frame, I could see lesions upon her skin. My eyes traveled from her wrist to her collarbone before nausea forced me to look back into her eyes. They were such sullen, sunken things.

"Poison."

The word was tangible as it traveled from our embraced fingertips to my pained breast. Our history, one I had not truly realized I had, manifested and left a searing mark there. Everything collapsed upon itself as Alcott stared into my weakened soul, and I learned what I had witnessed.

The patriarch, having committed his unforgivable act, corrupted the land we stood on, letting it ferment, adding more to it over the years until I would take his place. I could not believe the indignity of his final action, leaving me with this house of the dead.

A maternal instinct must still have lived within my mother's decaying body, as she pulled her hand from mine and caressed my cheek. If it was to console me, I did not know, but I felt abhorrence and guilt.

In this, I began to feel extraordinarily exposed. The visible nothings, hidden away in the rafters and nooks, watched me.

"I need to get out of here." My words were barely more than a whisper.

She lightly pressed her hand against my cheek to move my head, her other arm raising to point to our right, where I could scarcely see steps to a storm door.

I moved from her embrace, soon finding my head surrounded by the blue sky and warm breeze. My head pounded from the sudden brightness, my eyes taut, but I could see, at the tree line, a solitary person.

My thoughts of fleeing this place evaporated upon seeing them, although I did not know why.

Walking toward them with such a purpose as if we were to be reunited friends, I had not paid close attention to the hidden divots within the grass. I stumbled and fell, my breath knocked out of me as I collided with the ground.

My hands coming up speckled with rock and dirt, I gathered myself to see what it was I had fallen upon; it seemed to be some type of mound, and it caused all color from the world to drain away.

I began to dig incessantly, possessed by some maniacal power, as the dirt piled uncomfortably under my fingernails, smearing against my sweating frame.

Soon, my hands grazed upon something horribly mortal. Staring into the grave, I was met with a choking smell.

There lay corpses, all bones and rotted flesh mixed, their decomposing skin a necromancer's palette: colors of yellows, greens, browns, and purples that are not meant to be known by living men. Their eyes, if they were not burst to dust, were open wide like a bloated animal. Their bones protruded from one into another so that even if I had wished to count all that were buried here, I could not. The body of the murdered canine was heathenishly combined with the humans.

Face-to-face with varied death, I could do nothing but watch and wonder at how nature had brought these poor damned to their wretched state. I thought back to yesterday, when I had marveled at the state of this yard. A pang hit me, knowing the bees I had seen taking advantage of the greenery had been feeding on flowers of the dead.

Something moved behind me once more, but I could not bring myself to speak. My jaw was locked in disgusted and macabre awe at what my father had done.

I turned and rose, the loose grave dirt falling from me as if I were one of the dredged dead. In front of me, in the full light of the day, stood the matron Alcott and the vanished Nesbith. They looked less than human. Across Nesbith's unshaded face I could see the fracture of death, harsh wounds that would have threatened to bleed had he still held his mortality. My mother looked like a Thanatosian bride, with such a poisonous visage that perhaps she had melded with her cause of death.

Beyond them, I could see the swarm of the other victims, the visible somethings, that had to reconcile with their individual immortalities upon this unhallowed ground. I feared and wondered how many of them had truly watched me as I moved about the house, blindly following their tapping and running, peering into the locations of their deaths and hearing nothing. I wondered if they cared that I now wished to find them. I wondered, still, how many resented that I drew breath.

It would not matter soon.

A speck in the sea of the dead, one vaster than just the single grave, I collapsed amongst them.

At the foot of Alcott, I knew I would not rise from where I lay.

For the sins of the father…

I knew I would take his place in the village, one lost to the woods and time.

And I wonder, will Alfred remember us?

HE TO WHOM THE FLIES ARE DRAWN

MONICA NOWIK

THE ADDRESS HARRIET Farrow gave me didn't even register on the GPS—that's how out-in-the-middle-of-abso-fucking-lutely-nowhere this whole place really was. My phone tried to take me first to Alfred Station, then into Hornell before becoming completely confused and refusing to reroute. After I texted the woman, she told me that it would be the "little white house" near the Alfred Stables.

"It would have been nice if you'd told me that sooner," I muttered, squinting through my foggy windshield. I trundled along down Main Street, which gave way to a much emptier Jericho Hill Road. Whenever it got cold out, the heating in front decided to stop working and I could never get the windows to clear up. And it was usually cold in Alfred.

Screeeeeeeeech.

A woman walked out into the road—I slammed on my brakes. My tires slipped on the icy road and I swerved to the left, managing to stop myself in time before I hit the fence in front of the opposite farmland. Gasping, I hunched over in the seat, my body frozen in shock.

Tap tap tap.

Whipping my head around, I saw a middle-aged lady squinting in through my passenger window, her bony fingers pressed against the glass. I straightened up slowly; I hadn't hit my head or anything, and the airbags hadn't come up, although I wasn't even sure they worked. With one shaking hand, I finally reached over and rolled down the window.

"Didn't mean to startle you," she said.

I stared at her. "You...you were in the middle of the road!"

"I was on the side of the road." The woman jerked her head to the side. "There's another car coming, might want to turn around. You can pull into my driveway."

Looking behind her, I saw that she was pointing to the driveway of a little white house with an old but sturdy little fence around the snowy square of yard. Her face was devoid of expression, as if walking into the path of an oncoming car were the most normal thing in the world.

I suddenly didn't have a doubt that this house was my destination and that the woman I'd just almost hit was my future employer. Well, we'd see about the *future employer* part. We were off to a wonderful start.

I pulled my car into the gravelly driveway, glancing over at her the entire time to make sure she wasn't going to pull that stunt again. After my heart rate had subsided at least a little bit, I got out and looked at Harriet Farrow fully. Her hair was pulled into a messy bun, flyaways blowing in the wind; it wasn't quite gray, but it was getting there. She wore only a faded pair of slippers as she stood in the two-foot-deep snow, and over her house dress she wore an apron with a patchwork bear on it. Two mismatched buttons, one red and one green, served as the bear's eyes, and he was eating a jar of what I assumed was honey with one gingham hand as the other swatted flies over his head.

"I'm...sorry I almost hit you," I said, digging my nails into the palms of my hands. She wasn't even apologizing for making me drive off the road and here I was, saying sorry that her dumb ass was standing out there in front of an oncoming car.

Harriet's face was blank, watery gray eyes almost half closed. "I was expecting someone— I suppose that must be you. I came out to show you which house it was. Guess you had some trouble."

"Yeah," I said. I mentally shook myself. It didn't matter now; I hadn't crashed after all, despite Harriet's efforts to kill me before I'd even started work, and I needed to remember that the interview had started from the minute that woman laid eyes on me. I stuck out a hand. "Elizabeth —well, I guess you already know that. Liz is fine. It's lovely to meet you, Ha—Miss—Missus—" I stumbled on her name, not sure how I should address her. I'd hoped she would help me out, but Harriet just looked at me. "Ms. Farrow," I finally settled.

"I'll show you inside."

Without so much as acknowledging my extended hand, Harriet turned on her heel and marched through the snow towards the dull red door. There was really nothing else to do but trudge after her, soaking my Skechers in the process.

The house smelled old, like my grandmother's house. Not unpleasant, but not exactly nice either. It looked old, too: the overhead light in the foyer was dim, illuminating a small dark hall and a staircase leading upstairs. I followed Harriet through the hallway and arrived in a sitting room, mainly lit by the big window behind the frayed couch. Adjacent to the couch was a fireplace that didn't seem to be in use.

"Can I get you anything?" Harriet asked, pointing for me to sit on the couch. I did, seating myself across from a wooden rocking chair below a painting composed of abstract red squares interspersed with black dots.

"Um, no thanks." I was beginning to wonder if I'd walked into a *Murder, She Wrote* episode. "Very nice house you have here."

"It's not mine."

Harriet disappeared into the darkened next room; I guessed it was the kitchen because I heard her running a sink. She returned holding a glass of water and thrust it at me so that I was forced to take it before water spilled down my front.

"You have to drink water after a shock," she insisted.

I was about to ask her what she'd meant by saying the house wasn't hers, or maybe ask her where this child I was supposed to be babysitting was, but Harriet sat down in the rocking chair and resumed a rather awkward conversation.

"I have to tell you, I was glad you applied," Harriet said. She didn't cross her legs or anything, like a normal person would have who was comfortable in their own home; no, she sat on the edge of the seat, back stiff and hands clenched over her knees as she stared hard at me. "It's so difficult to find anyone out here."

"Ah." I shifted in my seat, wincing at how much the sofa crinkled beneath me. "Alfred is sort of in the middle of no-where, isn't it?" My joke fell flat, and I hastily gulped down some water.

A loud wailing noise assaulted my eardrums; after a second, I realized that it was a baby crying. Harriet jumped up from her seat, muttered, *I'll be right with you,* and ran back down the dark hallway. I heard thumping all the way up the stairs.

While she was gone, I wandered over to the fireplace. Several knick-knacks were arranged on the mantel: Matryoshka dolls stood in a row from tallest to smallest, solemnly guarding a few faded photographs set in seashell frames. There was also an empty silver ashtray with one singular dead fly lying in it.

"Just woke up from his nap," I heard Harriet say behind me, and I turned to see her bouncing a healthy sized little boy on her hip. He stared at me with huge brown eyes.

"Hi there!" I put on my biggest smile. I had heard that kids were more likely to respond if you smiled. Not that I'd really know or anything. The email, probably a remnant from all the job sites I was still subscribed to, had boasted of a gig that paid $20 per hour, two hours each day on weekdays, and when you see an opportunity like that you don't stop to think about whether you're the perfect applicant or not. "What's your name?"

"Damien doesn't talk yet," Harriet said flatly. "Except for the word *No.*"

My insides promptly curled up and died. Idiot. Kids apparently weren't fluent in the English language at ten months old.

"No," Damien echoed, waving a chubby hand.

As soon as Harriet lowered him to the ground, he took off at a fast pace, crawling towards the kitchen. His caregiver made no move to stop him, so I guessed that the kid was allowed to wander pretty freely.

"Your son is very cute," I said encouragingly, trying to make up for my blunder.

"He's not my son," Harriet said, and without further explanation she went over to a child-sized bookshelf in the corner, which held some plastic tubs of blocks and a few books. She picked up one box and showed me that it was filled with toys.

"He's not really that interested in playing with toys, so he doesn't have that many. He's much more content to play with the kitchen sink or bang spoons on the ground or crawl around and find little things he shouldn't be playing with."

"O-oh." I looked at the cracked plastic houses and toy trains missing wheels. "It seems like he's able to entertain himself pretty easily."

"Yes," Harriet agreed, placing the box back on the shelf. "You are mostly here for supervision. As stated in the description, you will be keeping an eye on him on weekday evenings while I am out. He usually goes to sleep around 8 o'clock; I'll show you where everything is upstairs next time."

I felt a little surge of triumph. So I really was the only applicant then - she was giving me the job right off the bat. That was great news, because I didn't think I could have competed with an actual experienced babysitter.

Damien crawled back into the living room and plopped himself in front of the fireplace, clutching a small plastic spoon. He smacked it against the wall with delight.

"If...if you don't mind me asking," I began, "What's your relation to Damien then?"

Harriet wasn't listening. "Damien, you're ruining the paint. Bad. Do it on the brick, there's a good boy."

I frowned, watching her. Something about the way she spoke to the kid made me feel...weird. Like I'd seen that interaction before somewhere else. Then again, I didn't know a single thing about child-rearing, so I wasn't one to judge.

Picking Damien up again, Harriet turned him to face me. "What do you think, Damien? Are we going to be friends with Elizabeth?"

Damien looked at me with those big round eyes. His mouth moved in a clenching motion, as if he were mashing up something with his gums. I almost pointed this out to Harriet, because maybe he was eating something he wasn't supposed to, but she pinched Damien's cheek, apparently unconcerned; she still wasn't smiling.

Not her house, not her kid – apparently, not her problem.

***

"And he starts getting ready for bed around 7:30, and he goes down around 8," I recited to a somewhat satisfied Harriet as she went out the door. Damien crawled around by my feet, surrounded by multicolored blocks. He had made a little whining noise when I'd taken him away from them in the living room, so the whole box had had to come with us.

"Hmph. I suppose you've got it covered." Harriet tugged on a pair of vintage white gloves. She was dressed from head to toe like a 19th century widow whose husband has mysteriously died and left her an enormous fortune: I'm talking the long veil, the floor length black dress—everything, except those white gloves which stuck out like weird spiders in a swarm of black flies.

I was going to have to tell Medha about this for sure; we had a ritual of making fun of employers.

Harriet had impressed upon me that Damien didn't need to be fed. She said that she would take care of every night. It was like she thought I was going to shove Cheerios down his throat or something—I got the point; the kid doesn't need to fucking eat.

"Damien, you be a good boy. A good boy, do you hear?" Harriet towered over Damien, whose attention was mostly focused on trying to fit an entire block into his mouth. I had realized what their interactions reminded me of: not guardian and child, nor yet adult and child, but one that was reminiscent of an owner talking to their dog.

"I hope you have a good time," I said with my best smile. Dressed like that, she *had* to be going to a party; maybe a really fancy costume party.

Resting her hand on the doorknob, Harriet turned her head to look at me. Her eyes were just dark shadows because the foyer was too dim to see through her veil.

"Unlikely to happen," she said, and on that comforting note, she was out the door, swallowed up by the darkness. I assumed, and have always assumed, that a car came to pick her up, because I'd never seen one in the driveway. Out in the middle of all that farmland, it would have been more than an hour's walk to the village. But I heard no car that night, nor saw any headlights.

"Okay, buddy," I said, turning around to face Damien, who was crawling around near the wall heater under the stairs. He looked up at me innocently. "Let's get these blocks back into the living room, okay?"

Damien just stared at me. His cheeks were puffed up all weird, and—

"What are you eating?" I raced over to him and grabbed his face, probably more roughly than I should have. "Spit it out!"

Damien, more out of the pressure of my hands than the instruction, opened his mouth and let something fall out. He'd chewed it up too much to tell, but I guessed it was probably a stray dust ball or something.

"We don't eat things off the floor," I scolded, picking him up. "Yucky. *Yucky.*"

Damien made a noncommittal "aaaah" noise as we went back into the living room, having forgotten about the blocks littering the floor. I picked a book off the shelf and we settled in to read.

Around 8, Damien fell asleep just as planned, and I gently placed him in his crib upstairs. The kid hadn't cried once all evening, which I hadn't expected but was grateful for. Except for liking to eat things off the floor, he was an extremely amiable child; a good thing, since I probably wouldn't have known what to do if he'd pitched a crying fit.

I checked that the baby monitor was on before wandering back to the top of the stairs. There, I paused, looking down the pitch-black hallway that gaped into oblivion on either side of me. I couldn't hear anything except the hum of what was probably the fridge downstairs; no cars passing by, no students yelling—nothing from the outside world. In such silence, I would have heard a deer stepping on a twig.

Perhaps it was because I didn't want to go back downstairs and be alone, even if my company up here was only that of a sleeping child, but I found myself stepping away from the stairs and moving down the hall. I hadn't seen any of the other rooms yet, and after all, why shouldn't I? Harriet wouldn't mind... probably.

The room next to Damien's must have been Harriet's room and was clearly in use, with skincare products on the dresser and an air filter whirring in the corner. When I saw that heavy drapes framed her bed, I snorted; it was comically dramatic. A soft red rug covered the floor underneath an intricately carved wardrobe in the corner. It was a stark contrast to the faded, clean-but-shabby rooms on the first floor.

A photograph of a young couple holding a baby stood propped up on the mahogany dresser; an ugly stain blurred their faces, but other than that it probably hadn't been taken more than a few years ago, given the picture quality. To the right of this was another photograph in a round glass frame, which seemed to be of a much younger Harriet. It seemed as though she had put a grainy, black-and-white Snapchat filter over it.

My phone buzzed.

How's it going??

Medha had to be updated every half hour. So I didn't get murdered, she said.

It's going pretty good. Kid went to sleep no prob. This lady's room is bougie as fuck.

Medha's three dots in the corner of my phone bounced as she typed.

Omfg. I wanna see.

Creep. Not right now you bitch.

Uhhhh okay Ms. Morality.

I snickered as I pocketed my phone again, backtracking out of Harriet's room into the hallway again. There were still two other rooms, one being the bathroom. I peeked in to see that an enormous claw-footed bathtub took up almost half the room. Badly chipped and scratched now, the tub had probably been a discount item even when it first had been purchased.

The fourth room and final room upstairs? Locked.

Disappointed, I withdrew from the door, but as I did, I heard a faint buzzing. Certain I was imagining it, I bent down towards the crack at the bottom of the door, where there was *definitely* buzzing. Maybe it was a heater or something?

A large black fly crawled out from under the crack as I was moving away. Then two. Then a whole cluster of them, buzzing angrily around the door, fighting to get out or to get in, I didn't know.

"Oh my god." I recoiled in disgust, involuntarily shuddering. "*Gross.* What the hell...?"

I retreated down the hallway until I was standing in front of Damien's nursery again. They were just flies—just some really horrifying insects, that was all. Flies were a thing that existed in the world, and sometimes they got into houses.

I turned to go back down the stairs.

"Ahhhh. Ah ah ah."

Damien's voice. He was awake.

"Oh no," I muttered, turning back. I opened the door

just a crack, hoping that maybe he'd fall back asleep or something.

Damien continued to gurgle, so I reluctantly pushed the door open all the way. By the nightlight plugged into the wall, I could tell he was standing up in his crib, clutching onto the side with one hand for support while the other arm flailed around.

"It's sleepy hours," I whispered, moving towards him, but I stopped.

Above Damien's head buzzed a swarm of flies. Every so often, he stretched out one chubby hand and snatched a fly out of the air.

Putting it in his mouth, he chewed, swallowed, burped, and then, looking at me, giggled.

I stumbled backwards into the hall, covering my mouth with one hand. I couldn't even choke out Damien's name. What would I have said, anyway? "*No, bad baby, don't eat the flies?*" It sounded ludicrous in response to what I'd just seen.

A loud *bang!* echoed down the hall; I gasped, clutching the wall for support. There was another bang, followed by a third. I twisted around wildly; I couldn't tell whether the sound was coming from nearby or from downstairs.

"Please," someone said. "Oh my god, please help us."

At the end of the hallway, a black shadow seemed to have fallen over the locked door. Then it moved, buzzing incessantly: the flies.

"Please, please, these goddamn *flies,* these *flies,* I can't *breathe—*"

"Who's saying that?" I yelled, taking a step away from the nursery. "Where are you?"

This last question was redundant, because I already knew where the voice was coming from; that door had been locked for a reason. Someone else was in the house with us.

"Please just come out and show yourself," I called down the hall, wincing at how polite my own voice sounded. I fumbled around my pocket for my phone and cursed myself for buying men's jeans with huge pockets. I finally pulled it out and tried to unlock it, but my finger was too sweaty for the Touch ID to recognize.

Damien was still standing up in his crib; now he turned towards me, wondering why his quiet room had suddenly been filled with noise. The buzzing of the flies grew louder.

Another *bang!* With a sinking feeling of horror, I realized that the noise came from downstairs. There was more than one person. I quickly swiped my phone to pull up the emergency 911 option, but my hands shook so badly that it slipped onto the floor.

"*Please!* Please, I can't breathe, the fucking flies, she did this, she did this to me—"

"What are you talking about?" I almost sobbed as I groped for my lost phone in the darkness. "Who are you?"

"My baby! Have you seen my baby? Is she feeding him what she fed me?"

I didn't answer. I had finally found my phone, and I waited, crouched on the floor like some frightened animal. The voice fell silent, and the flies, which had been crawling over each other and frantically smacking themselves into the door, slowly drifted back down to the ground, like a cloud of dust after the wind settles.

Bang!

"Elizabeth? Elizabeth, are you in there at all?" Harriet's voice. She was knocking on the door.

I bolted down the stairs, skidding on the last three, and flung open the front door. Harriet stood there, her black dress drenched; apparently, it been raining.

"I forgot my key," she began to say, but I didn't let her finish.

"There's someone here!" I blurted out before turning and running back up the stairs to be with Damien so that he didn't get kidnapped. "Someone's in this locked room, we should call—"

"Someone in this house?" Harriet started up the stairs after me, stony faced. "I'm not sure I quite understand you, Elizabeth."

"They must have broken in!" In frustration, I pointed to the door at the end of the hallway. "Someone's right there in that room, they're—"

Harriet reached the top of the stairs, quizzically looking from me to the door, before reaching for the knob. I started to warn her not to do that, but she rattled the knob in her hand a few times and pulled the door open as though it had never been locked, revealing a broom closet. It couldn't have been more than four feet in width, and it was emptier than my bank account.

"But... but the voice... the f-flies..." I stuttered, gesturing halfheartedly between the closet and Damien's room. "I s-swear..."

"Ah. Ahhhh, ah." Damien was still awake. Well, how could he have slept?

Harriet gave me a blank look. "I think I'll be attending to Damien now, as it seems he hasn't been put to bed yet."

My legs shook and I leaned against the door, staring into the contents of the tiny closet. My phone buzzed; a spam email popped up in my notifications, and below that was a message from Siri that said, "*I'm sorry, I'm not sure I understood that.*"

Inside the closet, one singular black fly crawled into a crack running along the wall.

A STUDY ON *ALIENUS TERRESTRIOSUM* IN THE ALFRED UNIVERSITY BIOLOGY DEPARTMENT

SOPHIE ECKHARDT

Bernard Prentiss
Alfred University

Abstract

Conducted on Alfred University's campus in upstate New York, this study focuses on the involvement and interference of the ghosts of *Alienus terrestriosum*, also known as ghost-aliens, in this institution's accredited Biology Department. My hypothesis is that ghost-alien involvement brainwashed the Biology Department into failing highly intelligent students because they are a threat to the entire ghost-alien race.

Introduction

Any STEM major in university understands the difficulty of maintaining a 4.0, especially with very opinionated "professors" and hefty research papers due almost weekly. When I came to Alfred University, I was managing well. I joined the debate club, went to the office hours of various professors, and actually found some measurement of joy in typing up ten-page papers on the effect of promoters on DNA replication or whatever the topic was that week. But my sophomore year, just around the end of February, everything changed. I was barely hanging on to a 3.0, and something inside me just knew that an external factor had to be at play. After testing for the presence of ghost-alien membrane fluids, I was able to conclude that ghost-aliens had infiltrated the Biology Department, brainwashing the professors into grading exceptionally intelligent students badly (B-C range) in order to discourage any attempts at what will eventually be, thanks to my discovery, the overthrow of the entire ghost-alien race.

Methods

To not only test but also confirm my hypothesis, I performed a biological DNA cleansing on the individual brains of selected faculty members. A total of four professors were used, with one professor acting as a control subject. Dr. Mitchem, Dr. Hartlieb, and Dr. Eickemeyer were selected as the experimental group, as they are all biology professors. My control consisted of Dr. Bradshaw, a professor of mathematics, clearly removed from the Biology Department not only by subject but by building. The groups were kept in separate remote locations and monitored closely through streaming cameras. Both experimental and control subjects had their parietal plate removed. This was executed without anesthetics, as these have been shown to interfere with ghost-alien membrane fluids (Braggart 1775). The independent variable was the presence of ghost-alien membrane fluid, and the dependent variable was the amount of bad grades given prior to the subsequent discovery of the ghost-alien membrane fluid. To identify the presence of ghost-alien fluid, samples were characterized by salty taste, a clear color, and watery consistency. All subjects were held for one week regardless of living or non-living state. Any necessary disposals were handled after all data collection. Contact between myself and the subjects was limited to feedings and procedures. Due to the possibility of ghost-alien vessel transfer, all living samples who remained alive by the end of the week were injected with potassium chloride as a precaution.

Results*

The results of this experiment showed the presence of ghost-alien fluid in all samples except Dr. Eickemeyer. This was determined through the criteria of texture, color, and taste. Of the three subjects with fluid present, none of them admitted to having experienced ghost-alien correspondences. They were clearly in denial. Politely asking the ghost aliens to leave their inhabited vessels was also unsuccessful, and no confessions were made. By the end of the experiment, Dr. Mitchem had been injected with potassium chloride, and all others had passed away somewhere along the process after initial fluid extraction.

Table 1. This table shows the experimental group individuals with corresponding observations of the cerebrum post-parietal plate removal. Trials were separated by a time span of three hours.

Experimental Group	Trial One Observations	Trial Two Observations
Dr. Mitchem	All factors (taste, color and fluidity) were identical to that of ghost-alien fluid	No change in traits from trial one Difficult to fully identify, as decay appears to have started
Dr. Hartlieb	All factors (taste, color and fluidity) were identical to that of ghost-alien fluid	No change in traits from trial one Difficult to fully identify, as decay appears to have started
Dr. Eickemeyer	Taste, color and fluidity not consistent with expected ghost-alien fluid	N/A Subject did not survive

Table 2. The below table shows the control subject with corresponding observations of the cerebrum post-parietal plate removal. Trials were separated by a time span of three hours.

Control Group	Trial One Observation	Trial Two Observations
Dr. Bradshaw	All factors (taste, color and fluidity) were identical to that of ghost-alien fluid	No change in traits from trial one Difficult to fully identify, as decay appears to have started

Image 1. The images above show the comparison in the surface of the control group's brains (right) to those of the experimental group (left). Photos were taken immediately after the removal of the parietal skull plate, and then again in intervals of 1 hour to monitor any reactions which were recorded in table 1.

Image 2. These images show the experimental (left) and control setup (right). Each respective basement was situated more than a mile from each other.

*Due to the graphic nature of the submitted images as well as a pending investigation, these are to be omitted from any future publications until either a court verdict is reached or they are able to be released to the public through other means. The image headings have been preserved for this edition, and a description of the results has been approved for publication needs.

Discussion

Overall, the results strongly support my hypothesis that ghost-aliens brain-washed and infiltrated the Biology Department in order to repress intelligent students like myself and prevent any future scientific success. The majority of professors who were found with ghost-alien membrane fluid were also the ones who had given me B-C grade ranges. Only one professor with the fluid, Dr. Bradshaw, did not, and that is likely because he was not one of my professors. I have, however, heard bad reviews from some students in his classes. This suggests that the ghost-aliens are infiltrating the Mathematics Department as well, which will be addressed in a future experiment.

The presence of these ghost-aliens on earth has already been studied by various science professionals. Former astronaut Helen Patricia Sharman stated in an interview that aliens not only exist, but that "it's possible they're here right now and we simply can't see them" (Eliot 2020). This undoubtedly confirms my suspicions as fact. Even more reliably, authors Trey Hamburger's and Mike Steven's second hand account of ghost aliens proves the presence of ghost aliens on earth, and, as I have now discovered in this study, in STEM programs on university campuses across America (Hamburger 2008).

Sources

1. Braggart, Dunce. "Effects of Anesthetics on various alien and monster brain slimes." *Journal of Alien Involvement,* 1775, 3(12): pp 11-27.

2. Hamburger, Trey. *Ghosts/Aliens.* Three Rivers Press, 2008.

3. Eliot, Lance. "Former Astronaut Suggests Alien Beings Are Here On Earth, If So, Maybe They Are Waiting For AI Self-Driving Cars To Emerge." *Forbes*, Forbes Magazine, 29 Feb. 2020, www.forbes.com/sites/lanceeliot/2020/02/29/former-astronaut-suggests-alien-beings-are-here-on-earth-if-so-maybe-they-are-waiting-for-ai-self-driving-cars-to-emerge/?sh=69abeb093bf9.

A campus walking path located near the woods.

Overshadowed by trees, Alfred University is built into the side of the mountain.

GLASS GHOSTS OF ALFRED

SHAN K. SUNDARAM

ROWING UP IN Scio, NY, I always knew two things for certain in my life: that I would go to Alfred University, and that Alfred, NY was haunted. These certainties came from my dad, an alumnus, a glass engineer, and a die-hard fan of *Ghostbusters* and *MythBusters*, as well as my mom, alumna, glass artist, and ardent Zen Buddhist. They repeated and reinforced these ideas throughout my school years. So, when I graduated from Scio Central, it was a short drive to the infamous college town.

As a freshman member of the class of 2015, I immersed myself in all things Alfred. There was more to do at the university than I could fit on my plate. Speaking of plates, I managed to survive the dining experience after persistent discomforts that eventually vanished when I discovered local farms around the town. I pursued all ghost stories, became one of the Forest People, went on haunting trails and trips, assembled my own high-tech Halloween decoration, and ate a lot of hot dogs. Just once, I saw the interiors of the Village Court for an incident involving snow, glass, and a blow torch.

What drew me to the glass were the contradictions I heard when glass was described: strong and brittle, transparent and opaque, liquid and solid. I wanted to explore the vast potential of glass. When the time came to decide my major, it was easy to call home and simply say, "I am doing glass." My parents were surprised that I wanted to follow in their footsteps, but I had always known that this was what I was meant to do.

Irreverent jokes and stories of ghost sightings became an integral part of our conversations among my circle of friends. Honestly, these stories took some of the academic pressure off. As I entered my junior year, I was blazing through my engineering curriculum, struggling in humanities and sports, and hearing some of the glass gods of the town speak in the classrooms of Harder Hall. Then, GlassArtEngine, an interdisciplinary course taught by professors from glass arts and engineering programs, happened. My circle widened to include cool glass arts majors. I discovered glass colors in my senior year. That is when things took a real spooky turn.

In my widened circle of friends, the chatter about ghost sightings in glass shops, laboratories, and hallways of Harder and HOGS steadily increased to feverish levels by our senior year. We heard daily reports of whirling motions in the hallways, unexplained glass breakages in the studio space, missing glass arts, and some scrawls on glass windows. We tried to dismiss these events at first, and then we tried to decode those scrawls to find some hidden, ominous message. We brainstormed over beers for hours and days.

One hypothesis bubbled up—what if there were glass ghosts? Suddenly, it all made sense. Of course, we could then see through them. They could be transparent as well as opaque. As a piece of glass, a ghost could vanish from sight when immersed in a medium of the right matching refractive index. It could stand firm as a solid but flow like a liquid when needed to. Like glass, it could use contradictions to confuse us.

As graduating seniors, we realized the clock was running out on us. We persevered the last semester. With graduation looming, an exciting job offer, and an uncertain future in hand, my mood alternated between melancholy and jubilant. Eventually, I settled for quiet, secret daily solo hikes up the Pine Hill trail in the early morning hours. This was my way of saying goodbye to Alfred in the last few weeks of the semester.

I remember that dry cold morning in May clearly. I woke up with a start; I thought I had felt a little swirl of air around me. As I contemplated and dismissed having a cup of morning coffee, my legs headed to the trail. I stopped at the foot of the path and looked up at the pine forest. I saw drifting, floating greens and browns like a smudged painting. It was like looking at the woods through a fogged glass window in a moving car. The colors appeared and disappeared randomly, then went still. I adjusted my bifocals to check again and swore under my breath, "those damn glass ghosts of Alfred!" As I reached the top of the trail and started turning back to descend, I heard a peculiar sound—the clang of crystals during toasts at formal dinners or the sway of chandeliers—circling around me.

As the forest was beginning to fade, I was pushing forward. But the whispering gallery followed me. I stumbled and fell. My trembling hands covered my ears. I frantically searched the rugged ground of the forest for something or anything. My fingers curved around a large rock and my grip tightened. I threw it at the shifting colors and sounds around me with all my might. After a moment of eerie silence, I heard a clear shattering of glass. I started running towards the end of the trail as the echo of glass shattering pursued me. The noise morphed into a cackling old man on his deathbed. I did not turn my head or stop. I was suddenly out of the woods, on my knees, panting uncontrollably. The view of Main Street calmed my nerves. I pondered: *"If a glass ghost breaks in the forest and no one is around to hear it, does it make a sound?"*

I never really found the answer to that philosophical question. After graduating and leaving the campus with an unsolved mystery, I kept in touch with my peers and others in glass science and engineering. The sightings of "glass ghosts" continue in the shops and halls of Harder, I am told, with no specific pattern or regularity. As I've moved on with my life, I've also learned to accept contradictions, and that some questions may never be answered. At times, though, my fingers still pause for a second as my hand reaches for a glass of wine.

Circa Twenty-Nineteen
S. K. Sage

I HADN'T EXPECTED TO see the old treehouse again after I graduated, but it never left my mind. I could recall every board's position, every knife-etched mark, every discarded joint or cigarette. It was our local haunt; every tree in those woods held the secrets and rumors we told up there.

Twenty years later, I found myself back on the summer-stunted sidewalks here, killing time while my daughter settled into her room in Barresi.

"You sure you don't want my Alfred shortcuts tour, Amy?"

She had rolled her eyes, smiling. "Dad, you gave that tour when I first got accepted."

"Can you blame me? I thought I was so clever when I found them."

"You're so clever," she laughed. "But my roommate wants to hang out for a bit."

She moved around the room, putting clothes in the closet and dresser, and it reminded me of when I first moved in. In twenty years, this place hadn't changed one iota.

"We're still on for the Jet, yeah?"

"Obviously! I'll text you, Dad. Don't worry." She hugged me.

Now on my own, I wondered where to walk first. The choice wasn't up to me, though, as I exited the building.

A voice called out, "Holy shit. Maurice? Is that really you?"

It had been two decades since I'd last seen her, but I would remember her face if it were the end of time. My best friend, the namesake of my daughter, stood in front of me, and I pulled her into a hug.

"God, Ami, it's been too long."

"Still as sentimental as always, Maurie," she said, but I could tell she was just as glad see me.

"You haven't aged a day," I said.

"You have." She punched my shoulder as she asked, "What brings you back to Alfred?"

"My daughter. She's gonna be an English major; can you believe it?"

"Good to know that that mistake runs in the family."

"Says the art major." I wrapped my arm around her shoulder.

Ami's laugh always echoed in this valley, and in that moment my mind felt pulled in two. I knew I stood there as a forty-two-year-old, but as we breathed in the summer air, listening to the chatter of students and parents alike, it felt like we were back in the late nineties.

"Hey, Maurie," she said, sensing my nostalgia with a sixth sense, "If you're not too strapped for time, would you wanna hike up to the treehouse?"

"It's still there, huh?" The buzz of everything coming back to me made my voice somber.

"A bit more decrepit now. No one really goes there anymore."

"Lead the way, Ami."

It was second nature to follow the road until we hit the trees and then to keep going. The light was a kaleidoscope here, forcing its way through the firmament of leaves and branches.

While we walked, Ami would get ahead of me, and I'd see how her dark hair never seemed disturbed by the sudden gusts of country air, how she walked with the same confidence as she did when we were younger. Whenever I was beside her, I could feel the years wane until I was in a hunger-wracked body with a mind for Austen and Emerson, quoting old Frost poems as we stepped over trap-roots and pebble cairns. I could feel the weight of a student's backpack on my shoulders, the straps digging into my flesh until it turned sore.

I took Ami's hand in mine, and I swore I saw my skin untouched by work and time. I found momentary solace in my temporary youth until I missed the sight of sunspots and scars, and then I untangled my fingers from hers.

"We're here," she said.

Looking up, I could see the treehouse, just as I had always remembered it.

The trees released the old sounds, and the light created long gone images. As she climbed, I could see the ghosts of the rest of them waiting for us—white canvases and contraband beer, the burning smell of the paints and alcohol giving us a headache—but we didn't care. We were young and happy.

"Maurie, are you coming?"

Ami's hand was outstretched toward me, the knees of her jeans getting dirty on the warped wood flooring. It was only there that I could see the air making changes in her appearance, the way she looked like she could float off if she didn't steady one hand on the half-wall. In her voice, I could hear the rest of them.

I started to climb, my hand reaching for hers, when I felt my phone vibrate in my pocket.

A smile crossed both of our faces, and I said, "I will come back."

"I know."

Ami followed me from the treehouse, our hands clasped the entire way. When we reached Barresi, I could see my daughter sitting on the bench outside. I felt Ami's hand leave mine, and when I looked to where she had been, she was gone.

The word *goodbye* hummed through the trees, a breeze that shook the leaves, leading me along the sidewalk and back to my daughter.

Mask On / Mask Off

Sophie Eckhardt

To whom it may concern,

The letter below is a piece of evidence used in the trial of Denero vs. Norfolk. It was found in a laptop file belonging to Justin Denero, a former student at Alfred University and a present patient at the Creedmoor Psychiatric Center. Drawing from my studies in the criminal justice system, psychosis, and the courts, I believe that this is a prime example of the dangers of seclusion and injuries without follow-up. By publishing such a deeply personal account of what some may call a mental episode, I strive to highlight the effect of a pandemic on students facing mental health crises.

On a small campus, with more green grass than bricks, there are student guards. They used to parade around in drab olive woolen overcoats to combat the frigid air of upstate New York. From what I remember, there were only a few of them, but now I can hardly tell. You see, they always wore masks, so it was easy to pick them out from the crowd. Their outfits were also a dead giveaway because they were from a different time. Now, though, we're all wearing masks, and the guards are no longer adorned in their standard army training corps uniforms.

My friends swear to me they were never there to begin with, but what else explains the unease we all feel on campus now? If there aren't any guards, we aren't safe. How can anyone explain away the lack of safety and comfort a college campus is supposed to supply us with? Though they seem to have simply disappeared, I know they haven't. For obvious reasons, I am writing this first-hand account to reveal and preserve the truth that is ghost guards patrolling Alfred University's campus.

Just last month, I had been out late, studying at a friend's dorm. Matthew Gallaghers, I think. There was a big organic chemistry exam coming up, and neither of us felt ready. After doing what felt like hundreds of practice problems, writing out mechanism after mechanism, I left his cramped Openhym room and headed back to my own suite across campus. Taking the long route back had never bothered me before, but that night, my paranoia walked right along with me. I can recall the forest beside me, and as I passed by the Science Center's top floor entrance, a rustling from deep within the trees kept me alert and walking fast enough to reach my safe suite in less than the standard 10 minutes. In my time at Alfred I have never felt so exposed and unprotected as I had in that moment. This is when I began my investigation into the guards and why they seem to have stepped out of the public eye. I have a theory that the only reason the guards gave up on their duties and either left or (the more likely situation) disguised themselves well enough to hide from the rest of us is because they're afraid as well. Having been through a pandemic involving influenza, the guards must have been shocked to leave on a round and discover that the trend was back. They were people at one point, and I'm certain that they are subject to the same trauma and post-traumatic stress that anyone else has to deal with. I've been trying to sympathize, but then I think, why should I? These supposedly loyal men are cowards for hiding. They *abandoned* us in *our* time of need. My friends think I'm crazy, but what's crazy about wanting to receive the loyalty and protection all those before me got to have?

I *know* the guards exist. I have seen them with my very own eyes. I have studied them, spoken to them, been saved by them, done all there is to prove their existence. The response is always the same, though. Everyone wants a picture, and I do not, in fact, have a picture. So what? How can anyone believe that I pulled myself out of the dead center of Foster Lake that winter night? I was all by myself, searching for the key fob I had dropped earlier, when the dark threw me off my path and I suddenly found myself crashing into icy water. Everything had gone black, and when I came to, all I can remember is the feeling of hands dragging my nearly lifeless body across the lake and onto the bank. Had the ghost guard on Foster Lake duty not been there, I would have died. It never mattered to anyone, though. It's always, "Oh Justin, prove it," or "C'mon man, cut the bullshit; ghosts aren't real, dude," or my favorite, "You're insane."

Discouragement is not in my vocabulary, though. I am going to prove their existence if that is all I ever get out of this institution. My plan is simple: reveal their faces under the masks. They couldn't have just disappeared. This plan is:

a. minimally invasive.
b. harms no one.
c. will be relatively easy to carry out while walking across campus with my doubters.

I am nothing if not organized. Below you will find a detailed schedule of what will occur over the next week.

Day 1.
Goal: Discover the movement patterns of the guards and note any crossed paths between them and myself on a regular scheduled class day.

Day 2.

Goal: Explore the campus at night after Honors class and note any "students" still walking around. This will be recorded as strange and sketchy behavior.

Day 3.

Goal: Reveal the faces of the guards to everyone who never believed me.

Names of people who never believed me, for reference: Abigail Smith, Jeremy Punnet, Stephanie Clares, Mathew Jameson, Dr. Eicker.

With the above methodology, I am certain I will be nothing less than the hero who uncovered our lost protectors through sheer determination.

Something went wrong. It was not my fault, but something very bad happened, and I fear I am the one who will be held responsible. If everyone had just believed me in the first place, no one would have gotten hurt. If they hadn't fought back and if that godawful ledge wasn't there, everything would have been fine. Just fine.

LET THERE BE LIGHT

S. K. SAGE

THE FOLLOWING (PARAGRAPH) clippings are from the March 8th through May 3rd, 1932 editions of the Fiat Lux newspaper at Alfred University, but have since been redacted. Infirmary updates and Opinions [To the Editor] are included amongst these. The newspaper clippings were sent in to the school historian some time ago. With the records of Alfred Police, Alfred University, and the local psychiatrist all being misplaced from this time, the following clippings are to be taken as fiction.

MARCH 8TH, 1932

Excitement reigned for a short time in the infirmary this week when Darla Hanson and Mabel Towner were brought in Monday night. Found raving near Five Corners, Hanson is being treated for extensive head injuries in Hornell. Towner was confined to the infirmary and will be discharged following a psychiatric appointment. Towner's condition is reported to be improving, following a confession that the "ghost" she and Hanson claimed to see, and be victim to, was likely a hallucination caused by stress and alcohol consumption.

MARCH 15TH, 1932

Mabel Towner remains confined to the infirmary by psychiatric recommendation. She is being treated for fever and migraines. Darla Hanson has been discharged by Hornell but has been admitted to the infirmary for post-treatment and psychiatric follow-up. Despite Towner's prior confession, both girls maintain their "ghost" story.

MARCH 22ND, 1932

Following the March 17th fire of Sigma Chi Nu, the infirmary is going to issue an announcement with the Alfred Fire Department at 5pm tomorrow on smoke and fire safety. Darla Hanson and Mabel Towner have been put under extensive psychiatric care following outbursts and melancholy. The psychiatrist, who has requested anonymity, is being treated for a fractured wrist in Hornell.

APRIL 5TH, 1932

The infirmary would like to make an important announcement that both Darla Hanson and Mabel Towner have been admitted into psychiatric care off-campus. As there has been harmful gossip surrounding what the girls have gone through, the infirmary would like to disclose to Alfred University students that authorities are now involved in the Hanson-Towner matter.

APRIL 12TH, 1932

To the Editor: —

It is my firm belief that both Darla Hanson and Mabel Towner have been unjustly put into psychiatric care. Regarding the authorities, I know who Esther Brooks is, and there is no cause for paranoia or intervention of the authorities. Although their story may seem incredible, and their lost time is confusing, I can say with absolute conviction that the girls are innocent of any nefarious activities, and as such they should be released from psychiatric care and brought back to live in the Brick and study with their fellow women.

A Friend.

APRIL 19TH, 1932
To the Editor: —

I am surely not the only one who has heard news that Hanson and Towner are being convicted of murder! Esther Brooks is not their victim; she is a friend. I refuse to speak with authorities, but I implore the rest of my fellow Alfred University students to petition against the current trial. If you want more proof that the girls are sane and innocent, I can say that I know this ghost they speak of, as I visit the Brick. She is quite normal, for a phantom. The only thing the girls are guilty of is being overly dramatic during a stressful spring semester.

A Friend.

APRIL 26TH, 1932
To the Editor: —

Thankfully, Darla and Mabel have been found innocent of the murder of Esther Brooks. As I had said, she is a friend, not a victim. She died in 1912, and that was some twenty years ago. If you wish to truly understand why Esther Brooks accompanied them to Five Corners in early March, you need only investigate.

A Friend.

MAY 3RD, 1932
To the Editor: —

I suspect this will be my last submission to this paper. Darla and Mabel have regained their place at this university, although the aura that follows them is as ghastly as the corpse of Esther Brooks. By demand, I have been asked to explain the story of Esther Brooks. She lived in the Brick, and, by a cruel deed, was murdered at Five Corners. I will not say who did this crime, as I do not know. Esther lives, dead, because her body has yet to be found! That is why she took the girls to the swampland. On behalf of her, to Darla Hanson and Mabel Towner: I express deep regret in causing you pain in the process. A dead girl's story is not one to be shared so intimately, it seems.

A Friend.

I Died

Audrey Buddendeck

"AND HOW WAS your college experience?" Dr. Gallen asks me.

I've told him about it a thousand times. And a thousand times the story hasn't been finished. I have to finish the story this time.

My hospital gown grazes the dirty tile floor.

I remember him asking me the day I was admitted. I told him the same thing I'm going to say now. I have to finish the story this time.

"It's quite simple really," I say. "Alfred University treated me well. I lived in the Pine Hill Suites for my first three years, intending to be a psych major, but here we are. The transition went fine; I didn't mind leaving the dysfunction that was my home. My mom hugged me goodbye, and my dad didn't even show up. Anyways, the first time I saw it was when I was in the bathroom.

"Saw what?" Dr. Gallen asks.

"Him. I was brushing my teeth when I looked up and saw the shadow figure behind me: a tall, slender man with a top hat. I felt like he wanted me dead. His eyes pierced my body even though I couldn't see them. Evil seemed to ooze off of him; my skin turned to ice, and my hairs became melting droplets. This all took place in about five seconds."

"And you trust your account is accurate, despite being here for a year?" Dr. Gallen has a habit of interrupting.

"No one forgets what they want to forget most. It happened again on Tuesday of the following week. I was walking home from eating at Powell when I felt someone staring at me. I turned around; the shadow figure was standing in front of the 'L' in the *Fiat Lux!* sign. This time it started walking toward me: steady pace, straight line. I could feel it staring me down, but again, I couldn't see its eyes. My whole body shook. The figure was closer every time I looked back.

"I decided to tell my roommate, John, about it. John said he had heard stories about the Brick being haunted, so he wouldn't be too shocked if the whole campus was. I tried to stress the fear that pulsed through my veins and express that this was no ordinary ghost sighting—it was a meeting with hell—but he remained unphased—"

"Did you often feel unheard? Were your peers not accepting of you?" If Dr. Gallen interrupts me again, I'm going to throw his clipboard out the window.

"I felt heard. My peers liked me. This isn't about my social life, Gallen; you asked me to recount The Story. Now, as I was saying, I went to the school historian to see if anyone else had had this experience. Turns out that there *was* a legend of a "shadow man", and she suggested, sarcastically, that I should see a psychic or request an exorcism from the local priest.

"I guess it's a thing: you see a tall, shadowy figure and people assume you have a demon attached to you. It's said that it comes through a Ouija board—at least that's what the historian told me, but I've never played with one. I blew off the story thinking it was just silly superstition.

"Sometime in the following week or so was when I first heard the diagnosis you have so casually pasted on my forehead, despite my vigilant efforts to demonstrate my sanity. That's when I decided to head to the Wellness Center, just to ensure that I wasn't hallucinating. I have the sanity to at least check on my wellbeing. They said I wasn't feverish, I wasn't lightheaded, I wasn't having trouble breathing, I hadn't hit my head; all signs checked out—"

"Wait, why did you dismiss the historian's suggestions? Why didn't you talk to a psychic or priest?" Dr. Gallen was asking for me to hit him.

Gallen has never asked these questions. My brain hurts trying to come up with an answer.

I have to finish The Story this time.

"I don't know, 'cause they were stupid. Gallen, do you want me to finally finish The Story or not? Anyways, the Wellness Center said they found it strange that I was having these hallucinations. They made a note in their files and told me to see a psychiatrist. When I asked why, the nurse casually said, ''cause it sounds like you're schizophrenic' and sent me home. The next day was when it happened: I was walking back from my Abnormal Psych class in Herrick Library, and again, there he was by the *Fiat Lux!* sign. This time was different, though. The usual feelings hit me—dread, chills, his eyes tearing my heart straight out of my chest and making me go cold—but he just stood there, and this time I didn't back down.

"I stared back at him. I asked him what he wanted—no answer. I told him to leave me alone—no answer. It was even more disturbing that I got no reply, just a stare. Then, his eyes began to glow red. The light radiated and impaled my chest. My body went cold; I felt light, airy, and heavy all at the same time. He lifted his hand so that his palm was parallel to my body, like he was making a stop motion.

"I felt nauseous. My head pounded; I could barely breathe. It felt like someone was stacking bricks on my chest."

I have to finish The Story this time.

"I felt my soul... escape my body. A glowing mass floated above me... I watched... the shadow man... absorb the... glowing light... I looked down... and my body had turned white... I was dead—" I can barely get the words out between breaths.

The figure appears in the doorway behind Dr. Gallen: right on schedule. I feel sick to my stomach. My hair stand on end and my skin turns cold.

The figure puts his palm out like he did in The Story. I feel it all over again: my chest stabbed by his glowing red eyes, my heart ripped out, and the cold, fear, and agony suffocating me. I'm not quite dead yet but not alive.

I have to finish The Story this time.

"I fell to the ground... I knew I was dead...he... killed me... Next thing I knew... I woke up in this gown... they said I had... a... seizure... but I know what... I saw... he killed me... I am dead..."

I fall out of my chair. The fabric slips underneath my gown and I feel the cold tile floor against the skin on my arms, legs, and left cheek. The figure is standing above me. Up close he is pitch black—a figure of nothingness, empty and yet full of evil. His eyes tell me he is succeeding in my murder.

I watch him lure my soul out of my body; the glowing mass appears above my head. I feel empty now. I can't move anything except my eyes. My soul enters his body through his chest that rises and falls with each breath.

The room around me has changed, too. I'm back at the *Fiat Lux!* sign at Alfred University. Campus is empty;

I am alone on the quad, dead on the ground, watching a demon steal my soul.

The figure lets out a maniacal laugh. His cackle fills the sky, and it's like thunder roaring above.

That's the first time I've heard him.

He is elated at his success. He is drowning in excitement and pride while I feel like I'm drowning in blood, yet I am not bleeding. I feel like I'm gasping for air but I'm not even breathing. I feel I'm alive even though I'm dead.

The shadow man starts running, then sprinting at me. I mentally brace for impact even though I can't move my helpless body.

Why is he running toward me? I am dead already. He has my soul—I am on the ground lifeless, so what more does he want? I feel his black mass of a body hit mine with piercing pain. So much pain, but no sound comes out. So much pain, I stop thinking. So much pain, I know this is death.

Everything goes black.

WE ARE STILL HERE

MONICA NOWIK

WE—THAT IS to say, those of Us who stood in the mist—watch the two walk up the sidewalk, take a turn, and head for the front door. It's difficult to see their expressions, because of the snow that swirls through the air like the breath of some giant creature lurking underneath the Brick. Even so, We—the Coroner is here as well—can see that they are giggling, cracking under the stress of midterm exams. The ice underneath Our feet cracks as well, which is sometimes the only indicator that there is any ice there at all.

"Good looking couple," the Coroner remarks. "I remember those days."

The couple is gone. Disappeared, just as We (*We* meaning all of Us) were thought to have done. They have been swallowed up by the dormitory.

Night is closing in around Us, though We do not mind it, for We can see in the dark, and even if We could not, the snow gives off an eerie glow to ensure that the students will see something—*something*—out of the corner of their eyes, never knowing what it truly is, never able to fully see Us.

We pass by the Campus Center: something that was not here when many of Us were born. We, who are far older than almost anything still standing here, look through the windows and see students rushing to get their mail, rushing to get dinner before an evening class, rushing to buy a last-minute textbook.

"They are always rushing," says the soldier, the place where his arm would have attached to his shoulder (the arm that was blown clean off in the first World War) glistening in the moonlight. "Have you ever noticed how they always seem to be rushing? Perhaps it is for the best. Their time will run out soon enough."

We walk down Allen Way, unseen. Someone stops, not quite looking at us, but aware of Our presence. She lifts her backpack higher on her shoulders and runs off into the night; she would be displeased if she were to learn that We are at the other end of campus, too.

"It's been such a long time since I've been seen," sighs the Nurse, something melancholy in her voice. "I suppose I'm much too faded... a photograph that gradually loses its definition."

"But just like a photograph," the Professor pipes in, "We do not simply disappear."

Yes, the Professor is right. We all nod in agreement, for something in what he has said has resonated with Us, something that stirs Our souls.

We are still here. Students. Professors. Nurses. Doctors. Soldiers. Townsfolk. We may be long gone, may be fading from the photograph of the mind, but We do not disappear, do not become non-existent, will not leave on Our own.

We are still here. Perhaps We have always been here. Perhaps We will always be here.

Who

                                                                    knows?

Not

                                                                        Us.